Resurrection Blues

First published in Great Britain in 2025 by Black Shuck Books

Cover design by WHITEspace
from an untitled photo of Pointe à la Hache
Photographer unknown
Courtesy of the Library of Congress

Set in Caslon by WHITEspace
www.white-space.uk

978-1-917173-07-0

Resurrection Blues

by
Marie O'Regan

BLACK
SHUCK
BOOKS

For Paul. Always.

The first time Marcus saw her was in Biloxi, Mississippi – in a rundown pawnbrokers' store in a piss-poor part of town. As he passed the pawnbrokers' shopfront, a glitter of reflected sunlight flashed across his face and he turned to see what had caught his eye. His grin when he saw what it was would have lit up a room. She was the sweetest harmonica you ever saw. Mother of pearl inlay on top of what looked like a walnut casing, all of it polished so hard she shone almost as bright as the sun as she lay there in the pawnshop window. Marcus could almost hear her calling to him.

He could just about make out an 'Open' sign hanging from the inside of the glass door through the dirt encrusted on it. As he pushed hard, the door creaked open and a bell sounded; a high, cracked note that somehow matched what little he could see of the store's dingy interior. Dust motes disturbed by his entrance ambled through the air, slowly sinking under the weight of the gloom. Marcus wondered when the last customer had ventured inside this place.

'What d'ya want?'

The voice was just as cracked as the bell. It spoke of age and destitution, someone weary of the world and all it held. As Marcus made his way toward the counter, he saw an elderly man – frail in the worst way, his pale skin loose and hanging on bones that looked as if they could barely hold his weight. This man was sick; his skin yellowing and his eyes watery. A few thin strands of white hair flopped across the top of his head, a last-ditch attempt to hide going bald.

'I said,' the old man went on, impatience creeping into his now-exaggerated tone as he carefully enunciated each syllable, 'what do you want? What are you, deaf?'

Marcus smiled. 'No sir, not deaf.' He gave a nod back at the shop front, and was careful to look bored when he asked, 'How much for the harmonica in the window there?'

The old man smiled: outrageously large, even ivory teeth appearing as his grin widened. Those dentures had surely seen better days, but then again, Marcus thought, so had he.

'That's a fine musical instrument right there.'

'Uh huh.' Marcus took care to inject just the right note of disbelief as he said this.

'It's true!' the old man went on, his eyes wide and just a little horrified at the suggestion he could lie or attempt to cheat a potential paying customer. 'Why, didn't you see that mother of pearl? That don't come cheap, son, I can tell you that.'

'I know, I know,' Marcus said. 'But it's a little worn, isn't it? A little old?'

'Why,' the old man said, and now his grin was back, 'surely that's a sign of quality right there. I can let you have it for five dollars.'

Marcus' eyes widened in disbelief. 'Five? You're crazy.'

The old man's smile narrowed, but he wasn't about to give up. Not when he was so close to a sale he could taste it. 'You don't get many harmonicas like this, son. This one's in a league of its own.'

Marcus nodded. 'I'm sure it is, sir. I'm sure it is. But five dollars? I can get one brand-new for 25 cents, if'n I want it.'

Now the old man's smile was gone. 'Sure, you can get one of those brand-new mass-produced thingummy-bobs, that's true. But not one like this, son. Do you know real quality? Can you see what makes something stand out, stand proud of the crowd?' He was on a roll now, and not about to lose a sale when it was this close. 'I can go to four dollars.'

Marcus thought about it for all of ten seconds. 'That's still too steep, man. Four dollars? I can't do that.'

He made as if to turn, and the old man was out from behind the counter like a flash. 'Now hold on, son, hold on; let me get the thing out from the window so you can see it up close. You'll see what I mean.'

He hurried up the aisle, all skin and bone, his white shirt standing out in the gloom, the breeze making it all too apparent how skinny he really was. That wasn't just being thin; that was being sick skinny. His pants flapped around his narrow legs like laundry on a windy day, held up by fire engine red braces.

Marcus heard the click of a latch and something sliding as the old man opened the panel at the back of the shop window so he could get at the display. Then the panel slid right back with a thump and the latch clicked shut again. The old man's breathing was a bit more laboured as he came rushing back, carrying the offending item happily.

'See?' he demanded, waving it at Marcus, gesturing towards his hand.

Marcus opened his hand, palm up, and the old man slapped the harmonica into it with a flourish.

'Quality work, just like I told ya,' he said. He stood there, sweating, wiping his brow with a big old chequered cloth handkerchief as his breathing slowed to what apparently passed for normal, in his case. 'Mother of pearl,' he muttered. 'Just like I said. Quality.' When Marcus didn't say anything, he sighed and shook his head. 'What are you, a heathen? Two dollars. Gimme two dollars and we'll say no more about it.'

Marcus stared at the harmonica cradled in his palm. It was beautiful. That might sound odd to most, he knew, but Lord how he loved to play… and this little thing in his hand wanted to let him. He just knew it. It lay there, the mother of pearl glinting in the light, just waiting – he felt like it was almost waiting to *breathe*. He thought about the three dollars in his pocket; the three dollars he had to make last. Ordinarily that would be fine, he could go for a while on three dollars; but he didn't know how much longer the job at Nevada Joe's (stupid name for a club in Biloxi, but people seemed to like it) would last. The audience hadn't been big to start with, and over the last few weeks it had dwindled. He looked at the dull glow of its inlay, hefted its weight, and made up his mind.

'I'll give you a dollar for it,' he said, 'and you know that's more than it's worth.'

The old man groaned. 'You're killin' me. A dollar? For that little beauty?'

Marcus said nothing, just watched as the old man pondered. Finally, he lifted a pained gaze to Marcus and nodded.

'Okay,' he said, 'I'll do it. I can see you'll love it, and that's got to count for something, right?'

'That's right,' Marcus agreed, and dug in his pocket for a dollar bill. 'It's still a good price, man,' he said. 'I could get one for a quarter of that, and you know I could.'

The old man sighed. 'You could,' he agreed, 'but not like this.' He stared down at the dollar bill that had found its way into his palm and nodded. 'Still, it wants to go to you, I reckon, and a dollar'll do, when you get right down to it.' He moved back behind the counter and pushed a lever, opened the till and put the dollar bill inside. As he pushed the drawer shut again with a *ting* he frowned. 'You look after her now, you hear?'

Marcus smiled and slipped the harmonica into his shirt pocket, where it hung warm against his chest. 'I will,' he said. 'I promise.'

The old man said no more. He reached out a hand, and Marcus found himself shaking it; ashamed for wanting to wipe it on his shirt when the old man released him.

'You look after yourself, sir,' Marcus said.

The old man nodded, a rueful grin spreading across his face as if he knew how futile that was, and waved Marcus away. 'Go on now,' he said. 'Make that harmonica sing!'

The light went out, and Marcus found himself standing there in the dark, alone. There was no sign of the old man. He'd managed to step out back without Marcus seeing him go.

'Guess you can't be that sick,' Marcus muttered to himself and grinned, a little mad at himself for not seeing how the old man had pulled his disappearing trick. He cast a glance around the now-dark store, noting the general shabbiness of the goods on the shelves, the peeling paint on the walls, and made his way back towards the door. It was a wonder the store was still going.

He took hold of the handle and pulled, surprised to find it now resisted. The wood appeared to have swollen in the frame, as if by recent rain, and he had to really tug hard to get it to open. Chips of paint fell off as the door swung wide, and Marcus blinked as he walked out into the open air. The sun had come out, and at this late stage of the day it was low enough to hit him right in the eyes as he emerged from the darkness of the store's dusty interior.

The harmonica shifted slightly against his chest and he smiled. As he walked back home his mind was full of what he'd play that night – if he had an audience.

His worry proved to be reasonable; when he walked into the club later that night there were no more than half a dozen people scattered around, sat in twos and threes around the stage as Ella sang the last few songs of her set. Ella was getting on in years now; she had to be nearly seventy if she was a day. And yet she liked to put on a show; to make herself up, wear her best dress and give her all for the audience, small as it was. She had a low, smoky voice, and she always kept anyone listening in the palm of her hand. Tonight was no exception. As Marcus looked around he saw the rapt faces of the audience and smiled – he had maybe thirty minutes before he was due on, and no one was going anywhere anytime soon. He turned and made for the dressing room; the other guys were probably already there.

As usual, he was the last member of the band to show up – he just didn't think getting changed into black pants and a white tux jacket should take as long as the others took.

The other three members of the band were sitting in front of the long mirror that ran the length of the dressing room, cups of coffee in front of them; though if Marcus knew them as well as he thought he did he suspected those coffees had more than a hint of Irish in them.

The oldest of the three, Earl, slumped back in his chair, a frown on his expressive face as he dabbed at his flushed forehead with a crumpled handkerchief. 'You're late.'

'No, I'm not,' Marcus replied, shrugging his shirt off as he moved to the clothes rail and reached for the clean white dress shirt hanging there. 'We've got twenty minutes yet.'

'Cuttin' it fine, boy.' That was Eddie, at forty a good fifteen years older than Marcus and not averse to reminding him of that fact as often as he could. He ground the butt of his cigarette into a battered metal ashtray, coughing all the while. 'What if you'd got delayed?'

'I didn't. It's fine.' Marcus' tone was growing a little clipped. Truth be told, the novelty of being able to say he was in a band was wearing off a little more each day, as he got tired of being put down by the older members. Since when did being younger mean he got treated like shit? What mattered was: could he play? And yes. Yes, he damn well could.

The last of the three, Albert, chuckled quietly to himself at the end of the row and sipped his coffee as he stared into the mirror at the faces around him.

'Something you want to say, Albert?' Marcus asked, hating how uptight he sounded.

'Nah,' Albert drawled. 'You're here before we go on, aren't you? That works for me.' He raised his coffee cup high, tilted it toward Marcus in salute. 'Here's to the show, right?'

Marcus grinned and nodded, doing up his pants and reaching for the white tux hanging on the rail. He smoothed the jacket down and felt in the pocket – then started to frown. He patted down his pants pockets, his shirt… nothing. Then he saw his own shirt draped over the edge of the counter and smiled. He could see the bulge in the chest pocket; he hadn't lost it already.

'What are you smilin' at?' Albert asked.

Marcus reached for his shirt and drew out that day's purchase. 'Look what I found,' he said, and showed the harmonica flat on the palm of his hand as he held it out to his bandmates.

Eddie and Earl glanced at it, nodded, and carried on with their own preparations. They could care less about some two-bit harmonica. Albert was a bit more forthcoming. 'Sweet,' he said. 'Where'd you get it?'

'Store over on Fifth,' Marcus answered. 'You know it? Real dingy, but this was in the window just shining away.'

Albert frowned and shook his head. 'Can't say I do,' he said. 'How far up Fifth?'

'On the corner of that and Hudson,' Marcus answered. 'Looks like it's about to close down, but I saw this in the window and just had to have it.'

Albert thought again. 'Nah,' he said, 'still can't place it.' He peered closer at the harmonica, his gaze thoughtful. 'Guess I'll have to take a walk up there, see what else they have.' He straightened up, frown fading as he asked, 'Ready?'

Twenty minutes later the four of them were up on the stage, playing 'Touch Me Light Mama' to an appreciative crowd. Although, Marcus thought as he watched them sway, 'crowd' might be stretching things just a little. Two, three, four, five, six… seven, nine… maybe fifteen now? Marcus frowned. He could see the people he'd noticed as he arrived at the club, still in their twos and threes – he could have sworn there'd only been six of them, maybe seven. He shrugged. A few more must have come in while he was changing, that's all. It wasn't like they locked the doors or nothin', and they could use the numbers.

He peered closer. There was a man standing just behind that elderly couple sitting to the right of the stage; his left, as he stared out. The couple were sitting there, holding hands, the smiles on their faces lit by the candle centrepiece as they swayed to the music.

The man behind them wasn't smiling. His appearance was darker, his skin the colour of smoke, as if he stood in shadows Marcus couldn't see. He was tall, thin to the point of being gaunt – and he was staring straight at Marcus as he played, the whites of his eyes glowing bright against the gloom, like lightning on glass.

Marcus faltered, unnerved by the man's unwavering attention, and as he hit the wrong note he saw the man blink out. First the eyes, then him. Just like that, he was gone, and for a moment Marcus lost his place in the tune they were playing. He took a deep breath, calmed his breathing, and tried to rejoin the others. As soon as Marcus hit the first right note, the shadowy man was back. Marcus stared, desperately trying to maintain the tune and not miss another note.

The man was clearer now. His eyes were closed, head tilted up to the ceiling, and he was swaying in time to the music – mouth open and slack-jawed. Marcus could see the shine of drool on the man's chin as the elderly couple sitting at the table were clapping their hands in time to the beat, oblivious to what was happening behind them. Marcus couldn't even remember what he was supposed to be playing. He was operating on pure instinct now, one eye on the man blindly swaying in the dark.

He recognised the opening bars of 'Mississippi Swamp Moan', their closing song, and felt the sweat on his back turn cold in an instant, as if something he didn't want to know about stood right behind him. Nearly there. He concentrated on playing, and listening to Eddie sing, and for a few moments could almost forget the figure in the shadows transfixed by the music.

Someone else had joined him now; a woman – smaller and stouter, her face similarly shadowed – but Marcus could see her smile all the way from the back of the stage. The joy of the music shone out of her, and Marcus found himself relaxing at the sight. Nothing bad could come of joy like that. Okay, they were weird, but they were here for the music, and that was all. Except… Marcus pondered on the woman's face for a moment, wondering why she was so familiar. Then it hit him, and he shivered again as a chill swept through him.

Missy Parker. She looked just like Missy Parker. Except she couldn't be. Missy Parker had died of influenza three winters before. Marcus' mother had cried for over an hour when she heard about the death of her oldest friend, and she'd insisted Marcus play something at her funeral. Marcus had liked Missy. She was kind, funny, and always swore Marcus would be remembered. 'You're gonna make your mark, young Marcus. You see if you don't,' she'd say, and then sit there giggling at her own joke, wobbling like a jelly as her shoulders (and the rest of her considerable bulk) shook with mirth. Marcus had played one of Missy's favourite songs, for her, and for his mother, who had broken her heart all over again when she heard it.

Now, as they moved into the last bars of 'Mississippi Swamp Moan', Marcus watched as Missy and her companion swayed to the music. Like the notes floating out into the room, they were starting to fade – smiling at him all the while.

Then there was silence, and in the few seconds before the scattered audience broke into half-hearted applause, Marcus found he was holding his breath.

'Hey, you okay?'

Albert was staring at him, his expression half-amused, half-concerned. 'What's wrong, Marcus? You look like you seen a ghost.'

Marcus laughed – a tiny, nervous sound – and shook his head as he wiped his harmonica dry on his jacket. 'I'm fine, just wool-gathering, I guess.'

Albert shook his head and continued on his way offstage, a cigarette already in his mouth. 'Well don't waste too much time here,' he drawled as he went. 'You've got a home to go to, you know.'

Marcus did know. And it wasn't much of a home. He slipped the still-warm harmonica into his inside jacket pocket and, comforted by its dull heat against his chest, started back towards the dressing room.

His footsteps echoed in the now virtually empty hall, and he marvelled once again at how quickly a room could become sepulchral. All it took was the absence of people for a stillness to settle that wasn't entirely comfortable; an echo to establish itself that spoke of other times and other places eager to find their way back into the here and now.

He looked over his shoulder just once before slipping behind the curtain, and saw an empty ballroom, chairs askew, smoke still hovering in the air – a blue haze of recent occupation. *But occupied by what?* he wondered, and shivered as he looked forward once more and hurried towards the dressing room to change back into his everyday clothes. He realised with something like surprise that he didn't really want to know.

As he let himself back into his room that night, he found himself noticing all over again how threadbare it looked. The narrow bed with its once bright, now slightly ragged quilt his mother had made for him; the creaking and splintered floorboards that were partially covered by another gift from his mother, a rag rug she'd worked for him with her own hands. She'd really loved him, he knew; would have given him the moon if she could, and he'd asked. All he really wanted was her back, or for time to be kind and allow him to walk it backward, finally reaching a home that still had her in it, her laugh lighting up the sky.

But that had been then, and it was a time long gone. Mama had died of the flu, just like Missy, not quite six months after her best friend had passed. Marcus had held her in his arms, holding her upright so she didn't choke as she coughed and spluttered, and he'd cried when she'd finally fallen still. His father had died long before; Marcus could barely remember him.

And just like that, Marcus had been alone.

He shook his head, mad at himself for allowing those memories to blast their way back after all this time. He'd spent the last couple of years trying to bury them, to lose himself in a new town, new time; with no ties to anyone. It hurt less that way, he found. And he could do with hurting less.

He took his jacket off and hung it on the hook at the back of his door, took the harmonica out of his pocket and placed it on the rickety wooden bedside table, where it lay gleaming in the light as he switched on the bedside lamp, seemingly satisfied with its night's work. He moved across to the window and closed the curtains, but not before looking down to see if anyone were standing by the streetlamp outside, gazing back up at him. No reason there would be, he told himself, and yet he looked. Once he was certain the road was clear, he pulled the curtains shut and turned back into the room, shrugging off his shirt as he did so. He plumped himself down on the bed, enjoying the creak of the springs in the iron bedframe as they protested at his weight, slight as it was. He lay there and stared around the familiar surroundings, wondering what it was that didn't feel right.

Everything looked the same: the lumpy, battered tan leather armchair that rested by the window – the one he liked to sit in on his days off, a glass of cheap wine on the little wooden table in front of it as he sat and watched the world go by. At night he liked to sit there and read whatever cheap paperback he'd bought that day at the pharmacy, from one of those racks they had outside. A cheap thriller, or a horror novel, usually; he didn't mind what it was as long as it drew him in and told its story well. The wardrobe stood in the centre of the wall facing the bed, leaning forward a little as it always did. Marcus had long since stopped worrying it was going to topple forward onto him. Something held it upright no matter how much it leaned, perhaps the not inconsiderable weight of its base, or maybe someone had nailed the damn thing to the floor, he didn't know. He was just happy it stayed put and wasn't about to break anything.

Other than that, the room didn't have too much in it. There was a cracked porcelain sink in one corner of the room, over in the nook between the bed and the window; a mirror hung above that, but there were no other pictures on the walls and the wallpaper was so faded you could barely see the roses on it anymore. It was beginning to peel here and there, too. But it was home, and it was clean if run down. He'd been happy here these last couple of years.

Tonight it felt different. It felt… uneasy, somehow, as if something was waiting. Waiting where, though, and for what? Marcus shook his head, annoyed at his suggestibility, and plumped the pillow behind his head as he leant back against the headboard. He picked up the harmonica and started to play. It was just random notes at first, played soft and sweet so as not to disturb the boarding house's other tenants, but it gradually turned into something more. It was a ballad of some kind, though Marcus couldn't place it, and wasn't exactly sure how it was he came to be playing it. The notes just came, each one layering itself sweetly on top of the last until the room was full of it, and Marcus realised he was crying.

He also became aware that he had company.

His mother stood there in the shadow between the wardrobe and the window; hunched down as if she were afraid to step out into the light.

'Ma?'

Marcus felt himself loosen – that really was the only word that fit. All his muscles turned to water, and he felt the strength run right out of him.

'Ma?'

She nodded: a tiny gesture, timid, but still she wouldn't come out of the shadows. Instead she raised her hand and hooked her finger; gesturing for him to come closer.

He knew better.

She sighed, then, and the walls of the room seemed almost to shiver, as if they were trying to increase the distance between them. *'What did you do, boy?'*

Her voice was cold, thin; a thing of the dark that had no place here amongst the living. The room smelt of dirt, now, like a garden after a good strong rainfall.

'I don't know what you mean,' Marcus said. 'I didn't do nothing, I swear.'

'You don't know, do you?' she whispered. *'That almost makes it worse.'*

Now he was truly scared. His dead mother was mad at him, or scared for him, and he wasn't entirely sure which option was worse. He wracked his brains for what he could have done that would so displease her she'd step back into the living world to try and stop him – and then his eyes widened as he thought back to the night's events and realised what it must be. The only thing it *could* be.

'The harmonica?' he whispered. 'Is that it?'

'*That thing is damned*,' she said, and now he saw a suggestion of tears on her cheeks, her face pale and somehow hungry. '*It calls us.*'

He thought back to the nightclub, to Missy and the man who'd stood behind the audience members, enjoying the music. Drawn to it somehow.

By him?

She nodded. '*You called 'em, right enough*,' she said. '*You dragged them back into the light whether or not they wanted to come. What for?*'

Marcus shook his head. 'I don't know.'

She bared her teeth at him as she stepped forward, and the darkness came with her. She was something more than his mother now, something had taken her over that was darker and more commanding than even she'd been; and he'd only ever had to be asked once to do something when her voice was doing the asking. '*There's a purpose to this*,' it grated, and nodded its head at the harmonica Marcus had dropped onto the bed. '*Don't you think you should find out what it is?*'

Marcus could only stare. His mother had been kind, caring. Not terrifying like the creature staring down at him now with eyes that were bleeding darkness.

It smiled, then. '*Thank the Lord you're seeing your ma, boy. Be grateful you're not seeing me.*' With that it turned its back on him and walked back towards the corner of the room he'd first seen her in. She seemed to trail darkness with her, tendrils of it weaving around her as if it was alive. Just before she reached the thickest part of the shadows, just at the junction of two walls, she looked over her shoulder at him. '*You can call me if you need me*,' she whispered, and now she was back to being Ma again. Her face was kind, her voice warm. '*You'll know how when it's time.*'

Then she was gone. The room was just his room, a little threadbare and a little worn; but there was nothing worse than dust devils under the bed, as far as he could tell. The light was back to normal, the room felt warmer, he felt… safe. Strange, that he wouldn't feel safe with his mother in the room, but then he remembered what she'd said. *'Thank the Lord you're seeing your ma, boy. Be grateful you're not seeing me.'* And he *was* grateful. He eyed the harmonica lying on the quilt with something like disgust, wary of even touching it in case something else appeared. It just lay there, staring blindly at the ceiling, for all the world as if it was nothing more than a normal mouth organ when it was clearly anything but. He snatched it up and dropped it none too carefully on the bedside table, flinching as it clattered onto the wood and came to a stop. It lay there, grinning widely as if daring him to pick it up and play some music (*can't you hear it already?*), and it was all he could do to open the drawer and scoop it inside, slamming the drawer shut on it as quickly as he could.

He lay back down and stared at the ceiling, his mind whirling as he tried to figure out what the thing pretending to be his mother had meant. He'd called those two in the bar? How in hell had he managed that? The drawer rattled and Marcus jumped, then laughed at his own foolishness. It did that when trucks or lorries drove past. It was traffic vibration, that's all.

Sure, a voice whispered in his mind, *you tell yourself that.*

It was a long time before sleep finally claimed him.

The next night Marcus was late to the bar, his mood visibly poor. He'd missed doing up several of the buttons on his shirt, one tail of which hadn't been tucked into his trousers. He growled a greeting at the other band members and drew the harmonica out of his jacket pocket before slinging it onto the dressing table and sitting down.

'What bit you?' Albert asked, the only band member seemingly willing to tackle him.

'Nothin',' Marcus said. 'I just didn't sleep well, that's all.'

'Well now,' Albert said, and his usual charm had slipped a notch. 'That ain't our fault, is it?'

It wasn't a question, and Marcus took a deep breath before he answered, taking care to make his tone noticeably lighter. 'No,' he said. 'Sorry. I'm just tired, you know?'

The other members of the band nodded and went back to their own muttered conversation. Albert watched him for a moment before allowing himself to smile, apparently satisfied with his answer.

'You need to take a nightcap,' he said. 'Nothing like a brandy before bed to knock you right out.'

Marcus smiled and nodded, knowing full well that what Albert called a nightcap was generally, in his case, at least a half-bottle of brandy.

Albert liked the finer things in life, and his shape and size reflected his tastes. He sat back in his own chair, chuckling as he stared at his reflection in the dressing room mirror. 'Believe it or not,' he said, wiping the sweat off the top of his bald head with a huge white handkerchief, 'I used to be as skinny as you.'

Marcus grinned.

'Don't go smiling like a fool,' Albert said, a grin creasing his own cheeks, 'it'll happen to you one day, you see if it don't.'

Marcus sighed, and stared at his stringbean reflection in the same mirror. They looked incongruous, sat there side by side. One little, one large, features not too dissimilar all the same. They shared a similar wide smile, eyes that crinkled shut when they really laughed; and they laughed together often, having become good friends in the last year or so. 'Mama always said I didn't eat enough to keep a bird alive,' he said, 'can't see me getting big if I keep that up.'

Albert shook his head, the smile slipping just a little. 'My ma told me the same thing,' he said, and now the smile slipped a little more. ''Course, there wasn't that much to eat when I was growing up, and I grew fast, so how was she to know I'd spread *out* when I stopped growing *up*?' He stared down at his belly, straining against the buttons of his shirt, and shook his head. 'You mark my words,' he said, 'it'll come to you too, one day. You stop growing up, you start growing out. That's just what happens.'

Vaguely, Marcus was aware of the MC's voice in the distance, announcing their arrival. He joined the others and scraped his chair back, hooked his jacket off the back of the door and slipped his harmonica carefully into his pocket before bounding on stage with a wide smile plastered across his face, ready to play once more.

There were more of them this time. For the first few songs everything had been normal. People seemed to be enjoying themselves, swaying along to the music as they chatted and drank – a few even danced. The band relaxed into the music, having as good a time as their audience, and the night flew by.

Towards the end of the night, though, the music slowed and so did the crowd. Two or three couples stood entwined on the dance floor, moving slowly to the music. There were a handful of people dotted around the room, sitting talking or just drinking – and behind all that, Marcus saw there were now four or five that had been called by his playing. They stood, swaying, silently judging it seemed to him, at the back of the room. He saw Missy Parker, standing mournfully in their midst, clutching her big old handbag to her chest as she mouthed something at him he couldn't hear. Beside her was the man he'd seen with her the previous night, and now there was a young couple – the girl with bright red hair and equally vivid lipstick, grinning like a clown at him even as he saw the crater in the side of her head where someone had shot her. She was joined by a young man, his face nothing but pulp, a shock of black hair sitting atop that mask as if it were the only thing left alive about him. A little girl stood just in front of them, her hair as bright as that of the woman who was surely her mother. She looked perfect, no wounds Marcus could see – until she turned her head to smile up at her mother and he saw that the back of her head was gone; the edges of the wound clotted black with dried blood.

Marcus faltered, the music jarring for just a moment. He saw his bandmates turn questioning looks his way once more, but worse: he saw the dead ripple. They flickered out just for a moment, then stood there just as they had before, swaying in time to the music, staring at him all the while.

He took a deep breath and resumed playing, careful not to miss any more notes. None of their living audience seemed to have noticed, they were intent on their drinks or each other. The other guys hadn't missed a note, just kept playing. Drink and desire had taken care of the rest.

The final notes floated mournfully into the air; the last song was almost always sad, Marcus thought, and wondered why that was. He watched the entwined couples disengage and thought now that maybe he understood, after all. When you were sad you wanted something to cling to, and what better than your honey at the end of the night? He found himself wishing he wasn't alone, wishing he had someone, and as if by magic his mother appeared at the front of the group behind the dancers.

She was crying. She stood there, between Missy Parker and the middle-aged man that seemed to accompany her each time, and she held out her hands to her lost son even as her shoulders shook with the effort of the sobs forcing their way out of her bony chest. As the music stopped, the company of the dead started to fade, and the last Marcus saw of them was Missy placing a rotting arm around his mother's shoulders. Scant comfort, he was sure, but the most she could manage now.

Then they were gone, and he and the guys were packing up their things and heading back to the dressing room even as the last straggling members of the audience were making their way outside and then on home. The world was a weird and wonderful place, Marcus found himself thinking. And sometimes it was downright terrifying.

As he walked home, he stared up at the bone-white moon, leaves scudding across its surface in the rising wind, and wondered what he'd let loose by buying that

God-forsaken harmonica. He resolved to go back the very next day to the store where he'd bought it, and to ask the seller where it was from and how come he'd sold such a thing to an unsuspecting member of the public. He'd demand a refund, he decided, and God help the old man if he argued.

Something crunched underfoot, not far behind him, and Marcus whirled round to see what was following. There was nothing there. The road was empty, save for the day's detritus being blown across the street here and there: a tattered newspaper, a paper bag. A bottle was rolling down the street somewhere nearby, tinkling end over end as it went.

The street was long and wide, running straight behind him for some distance before the next intersection. He could see lights in the odd window, hear people arguing in an apartment somewhere close… but there was no one out on the street with him.

Someone laughed just behind him, and Marcus found he couldn't bring himself to look. He felt cold breath against his neck and shivered, shrugging the collar of his jacket higher as he willed himself to turn.

Nothing. He was alone on a deserted street in the middle of the night, and he'd never wanted to be safe in his room more than he did right at that moment. He felt a drop of liquid hit his face, then another, and another, and then the skies had opened and he was running for home, intent on getting out of the downpour, all thoughts of who or what had been tormenting him forgotten, at least for now.

His room was wet. He stood shivering in the doorway, rain soaking through his clothes – and there was a pool of water in the middle of the room before he'd even stepped in. No. *Two* small pools of water, next to each other, for all the world as if someone's wet shoes had stood there just moments before.

It was cold in there. He'd thought he was cold running through the streets at night soaked through to the skin, but now he felt as if he was inside an icebox. His skin prickled and shrank back from the rapidly dropping temperature, and he felt the air rasping against the inside of his throat and chest as he sucked air in.

'Ma?'

Now why had he asked that? The room was empty, save for those two tell-tale puddles in front of him. And even as he watched, they shrank into the gaps between the floorboards, until a moment later they might never have been there at all.

The room was starting to warm up, now that they were gone. Marcus stood there, waiting, for what felt like hours but could only have been a minute or two, but no one materialised. Shaking his head, he took his soaked clothes off and hung them on hangers by the window before towelling himself off and getting into a pair of pyjamas. He left his room briefly to head to the kitchenette down the hall and make himself a cup of coffee, some toast. He took the food and coffee to his room and placed them on the bedside table before sitting on the bed, swinging his legs up onto it and stretching out. He thought about the evening's events: the people in the dancehall just dancing away, chatting and laughing or just drinking and talking at their tables – and the dead people standing at the rear of the hall, swaying in time to the harmonica like snakes following the charmer's flute. Ma said he'd called them, and he thought that maybe that was true. But he hadn't meant to, and he wondered if that mattered.

'It doesn't matter at all,' someone whispered next to his ear, and then something was on top of him, pressing him down against the bed with the weight of what felt like a good-sized man, with breath that smelt of swamp gas, and worse.

'Who are you?' he shouted, and felt a hand close around his throat, cutting off further noise.

'I am who I am, son,' it said. *'That's all you need to know.'*

Marcus whimpered, the most sound he could now manage to make. Abruptly, the weight lessened, and he found he could breathe more easily. He didn't risk talking though, not yet.

'That's right,' the voice said, and now it sounded like his mother once more. Plainly it wanted to keep him on its side, not terrify him into uselessness. *'I just want to talk to you, son, that's all. We can talk, can't we?'*

And just like that, there she was. His mother sat on the side of the bed, one finger playing in her hair just as she'd always done when she was nervous. This wasn't his mother, he knew that much now, at least, but just seeing her there calmed him down enough to listen, and that was always the aim, of course.

'You called 'em again,' it said.

Marcus nodded. 'I didn't mean to.'

'That don't matter. You called 'em, but you don't know what to do next, do you?'

'No,' Marcus replied. 'I don't.'

'Where did you get the harmonica, son?'

Marcus saw it was in his mother's hand, lying flat on her palm as she offered it to him. He shrank back, not wanting to touch it. 'There's a store…' he started.

'*Oh yeah,*' she said. '*I know the one.*'

How could she? He couldn't remember its location now himself, let alone tell her where it was. And yet she did know something, he could tell.

'*That man could sell stars to the moon,*' his mother said, and now there was a grim smile on her face. She stared at Marcus, her expression kind on the surface… but there was something else underneath. Something that Marcus felt wouldn't so much as twitch if it felt the need to rip his face off.

'I could take it back,' he offered, and tried not to look crestfallen when she started to laugh fit to bust a gut.

'*Whoo,*' she said, '*that's a good one. You think he'd still be there, son? Hell, do you think the* store *would still be there, right where you left it?*'

Marcus shook his head, trying to retain at least a little of his dignity if he could. 'I guess not,' he said. 'But why did he sell it to me, then? If you know so much, tell me that, why don't you?'

Now she wasn't laughing. She wasn't even smiling. Her face fell and set into hard, grim lines as she frowned at him. There was something like coal glowing in her eyes, and that fire was growing fast.

'*I guess he knew a fool when he saw one,*' she snapped. '*He wasn't wrong, was he? Look what you did!*'

'How was I supposed to know?' he said. 'It's just a harmonica, for God's sake!'

Except it wasn't, and he knew that now. Somehow, the harmonica had the power to call the dead to him. He knew they wanted something from him, the way they swayed to the music and held their arms out to him, lost in the music though they were. What he didn't know was what that something was.

'*That's why I'm here,*' she said, reading his mind. '*Now hush up and listen.*'

Marcus felt the pressure lift off him completely, and he pulled himself upright once more to lean against the wall behind the bed. His breathing was ragged, and his chest felt as if a great weight had just been lifted off it. He hurt all over.

'*That harmonica used to belong to a man,*' the woman who wasn't his mother said, and she crossed one leg over the other and leaned forward, her eyes eager now. She *wanted* to tell this story, she wanted the world to know, and she was going to take her sweet time doing it.

'*His name was Louis DuPaul, and he was a busker right here in Biloxi. He'd sit on a street corner, cap in front of him, and he'd play. Oh, he could play, alright; people rarely passed by without dropping a coin or even a note in that cap, and come evening he'd have plenty to go and buy a good meal, a bottle of wine… and still have enough to take home.*'

'Where did he live?' Marcus asked, and was rewarded with a flash of fire from those coal-black eyes. He shut up, and waited for her to tell this tale in her own time.

'*He had a place outside town,* she said. *No one knew exactly where, but the story went that it was nice. A house, a wife, even a couple of children. He could afford to keep them right well, just from playing that harmonica on the street every day.*

'*Then one day he was gone, no one knew where. People didn't take so much notice at first, of course, but then news came that a house on the outskirts of town had burnt down, taking everyone inside with it – the harmonica player, his wife, children. All gone. Folk weren't the same after that, somehow. They missed the music, you see?*'

Marcus didn't. This was starting to sound more than a little far-fetched to him, and once again he found himself wondering who this creature was, that took on the semblance of his mother and tried to make him see… what, exactly?

'*You will,*' she said, and now her voice was sad. More than that, it was starting to sound lower in tone, deeper; and the creature at the end of his bed no longer resembled his mother. It was a man, blackened by fire, skin crisped and split, oozing fluids from the wounds all over his body. He smiled, and the teeth were still startlingly white in that face, even though the eyes were pretty much gone – just like poached eggs, soft and kind of milky. Marcus supposed they probably weren't seeing much of anything anymore.

'*You'd be wrong there, son,*' the man said, and now his voice was strong and firm once more. '*I see everything just fine.*' He leaned forward, staring into Marcus' face, his expression intent even though his eyes seemed clouded over. '*I see you, for starters.*'

His hands shot out and gripped Marcus by the elbows, pulling him forward until their faces were almost touching.

Marcus yelled, tried hard not to breathe as the stench of burnt meat and putrefaction was overpowering now; he didn't know how he could have missed it before.

'*You want to know what to do?*' it croaked. '*Bring 'em home, that's what. Bring 'em home, to me! You can keep the 'monica till then.*'

And then he was gone, and the room was empty save for Marcus, choking on the stench that still permeated the air. Marcus brushed himself down, frantic, sure he was never, ever, going to get rid of that smell. It had seeped right into him, somehow, become a part of him. At least until he did what that *thing* (Louis, his mind whispered; its name was Louis) wanted him to do. Bring the dead home.

But where was that?

Marcus laid low for some days after that. He stayed in his room until he was starving, then went out for food and scuttled right back. He spoke to no one, kept his head down, ate and drank fast. And he stayed a healthy distance from that damned harmonica – in fact it was currently residing at the back of the top shelf inside his wardrobe, behind a stack of blankets for the winter. And there it would stay, he decided, until he could figure out how to get rid of it safely. Every now and then he'd hear a rattle, or the light in the room would change for no reason that he could see, and he'd leap to his feet, terrified. He'd then search the room, beginning with the damn wardrobe, until he was convinced everything in there was okay – and only once he was sure would he make his way to the window and search the street outside, watching its comings and goings for some twenty minutes or more, until finally he'd sit back down on the bed and prop himself up against the headboard to keep watch, all the while telling himself not to be such a damned fool.

Towards the end of this sequestration, Marcus knew he might not be a fool, at least not entirely, but he was certainly damned. Night after night, Louis would whisper in his dreams, cajoling him to play the harmonica, play that tune again. It wanted to be played, it *needed* to be heard again. The dead were waiting, and they wouldn't wait for long.

Marcus would wake up from these dreams sweating, a cry on his lips as he forced himself upright, convinced beyond any shadow of a doubt that Louis would still be there, sitting on the edge of his bed, leaning over him and wafting his charred breath down into Marcus' face as he whispered to him.

He never was. Marcus didn't know whether that made him lucky or crazy. Or both. In the end, it didn't matter which, if he couldn't make it stop.

After a week of this, as if he knew all might be lost, Louis left him alone. One night Marcus went to bed and slept like he hadn't done in years. He closed his eyes and it seemed like a moment later he opened them again to bright sunshine, feeling fine. Better than fine; he was hungry, and had more energy than he'd had since all this business had started. For a moment, Marcus paused and thought about why it had stopped, why Louis had left him alone for once – then he decided he didn't care. He'd slept long and hard, and he felt better. Maybe it *had* all been in his mind. His mother had always warned him against pursuing a career as a musician. 'Those people are feckless, Marcus,' she'd say, 'they're not regular, like you and me. You and me need to know where the next meal's coming from, and that the roof over our heads is always goin' to be there.' She'd mutter this again in various combinations while she served a meal, or did the laundry, or even while they were sat together in the evenings, listening to music on the old gramophone that had belonged to her mother before her.

Marcus had smiled and nodded, all the while promising himself that music was where his passion lay. Music would make him a living, and a handsome one at that. And now here he was, nearer thirty than twenty, all alone in the world and not worth a dime. 'Guess Ma had the last laugh after all,' he muttered to himself. 'Now I'm seeing ghosts.' He resolved to get a job, a steady one, and start rebuilding his life. 'You're getting too old for this, Marcus,' he told himself. 'You need to stand up, admit to it, and make a fresh start.'

He flinched when a knock came at the door, then laughed, ashamed of himself. He stood, walked across and opened the door to find Albert standing there, a worried expression on his face.

'You okay?' Albert asked. 'I know you called in sick, but it's been a while since we saw you now.'

Marcus nodded, moving back and opening the door wider to allow Albert into his room. 'I'm getting there. Sorry I let you guys down.'

'That's alright,' Albert said, his gaze taking in the rumpled bedclothes, the empty whiskey glass on the table and the two-thirds empty bottle beside it. He saw the tightly drawn curtains and crinkled his nose at the oppressive atmosphere in the kid's room. He walked across to the window and drew the curtains wide, pulled the window up and locked it in the half-open position to let some air in. 'There,' he said. 'Fresh air will perk you right up.'

He turned towards Marcus, smiling, and stopped when he saw the boy's face. Marcus couldn't hide his fear, but knew Albert wouldn't see what he was afraid of. He watched as Albert walked towards him, hands raised open-palmed in a calming gesture.

'You alright?' he whispered.

'I'm okay,' Marcus answered, ashamed of his overreaction. 'Don't know what spooked me there, I'm sorry.'

'That's alright, we all get spooked sometimes,' Albert said, a reassuring smile on his face. 'Tell you what, why don't we step out to the café over the road and get an iced tea, have a talk. That sound good to you?'

Marcus nodded, looking shamefaced now. 'That sounds fine to me, Albert.'

'My treat,' Albert said, and started to tidy a few things up, picking clothes off the floor, straightening a chair. 'You go on and get ready now, then we'll go.'

Marcus hesitated for a moment, ashamed to see his friend clearing up after him, but then Albert shooed him away and he grinned, making for the bathroom. An iced tea in the open air sounded pretty good. It sounded wonderful in fact.

He emerged from the bathroom some ten minutes later, fresh and awake, to find Albert had laid out clean clothes on the bed for him. He was sitting in a chair by the window, watching the comings and goings on the street below, a smile on his face as the sounds of a busy Saturday wafted up. The curtains were blowing gently in the breeze, and the sun looked to be shining out there.

'Get those on,' Albert said, gesturing at the fresh clothes. 'Then we'll take a walk.'

Marcus smiled at him and dressed quickly, suddenly aware of how hungry he was. He couldn't rightly remember the last time he'd sat down to a proper cooked meal, not just a sandwich and a glass of milk or some such. He cast a furtive glance at Albert as he got dressed, wondering if the man knew what he'd been doing, what he'd been hiding from. He had a feeling he'd soon find out.

Twenty minutes later they were sitting at a small round cast iron table on the street just outside the café, squinting in the sunlight and watching the world go by while they waited for their food and iced tea.

Albert sat back, sighing as he stretched his long legs out under the table. 'So,' he said, 'want to tell me what's really going on?'

Marcus' smile disappeared. He sat there for a moment, letting the air play with his hair, freshen his skin, then leaned forward and rested his elbows on the table, hands clasped as he gazed seriously at his friend. 'I don't know how to explain it,' he said. 'It's… it's weird, is what it is.'

'Try me.' Albert no longer looked like a genial older friend, a mentor. Now he looked angry, almost. Worried, certainly. 'You've been gone over a week now; no word as to how you're doin', even what's wrong, really. So tell me. I'm here, ready to listen.'

'You know that harmonica I bought?' Marcus started, and was surprised to see Albert's lips tighten at its mention.

'You mean the one that's been raisin' the dead?' he asked.

Marcus' jaw dropped open, and he stared at his friend in disbelief. 'You knew?'

'What do you think I am? Stupid?' Albert was angry now; he leaned forward and wagged his finger at Marcus, all semblance of geniality long gone. 'I saw 'em the first time you played. Didn't you notice?'

'N…no,' Marcus stammered. 'I must have been too busy tryin' to figure out what I was seeing myself, I guess. I'm sorry, Albert.' Then he sat straight, indignation starting to overtake the shame he'd felt. 'Hang on, though,' he said, 'why the hell didn't you say nothing?'

'I thought you knew!' Albert shouted, and then stopped and took a breath, looking around them. People were starting to turn, to see what the fuss was, and whether it was worth listening to so they could spread it around later. He composed himself and sat back again, clearing his throat. 'I thought you knew what you were doin',' he continued in a more level tone, although his anger hadn't gone away entirely. There was an edge to his voice that let Marcus know he wasn't out of the woods just yet. 'I mean, why the hell would you play something like that if you didn't?'

'I just thought it was a harmonica, that's all,' Marcus answered, and now his voice was wobbling, just a little, at the thought that maybe he had been as stupid as his ma thought, after all. 'How come you could see 'em and the others couldn't?'

The waitress had arrived at the table with their food and tall glasses of iced tea, glistening with moisture. She set the plates of food down, the drinks in the centre of the table, and smiled at them before leaving. 'Can I get you anything else, fellas?'

'No, ma'am,' Albert answered, as Marcus shook his head. 'But thank you, these look wonderful.'

She beamed at him. 'You want anything else you just wave, okay?' Then she was gone, and Albert was watching her retreat with a smile on his face.

'I guess you're not *that* old, huh,' Marcus said, and grinned at his friend.

Albert looked taken aback, then laughed, and everything was alright again. 'Damn right I'm not that old,' he said, and both men laughed.

The food was indeed delicious; heaped chicken and bacon sandwiches, piping hot, with fries on the side. Both men did nothing but eat for the next five minutes, washing mouthfuls down with the iced tea until their hunger was satisfied, at least a little.

Marcus stopped halfway through his meal, belched, and sat back, smiling. 'Thanks Albert,' he said, 'I needed this.' He took another bite of his sandwich and chewed, content with the world, at least for now.

Albert looked up, a bunch of fries in his hand. 'I know you did,' he said. 'You couldn't stay cooped up in there much longer; you'd have gone out of your mind with it all.' He cast a glance back over Marcus' shoulder and a frown glided across his face – gone before Marcus could even be sure he'd really seen it.

Marcus turned to follow the direction of Albert's gaze and shivered. The older man had been staring up at his apartment window; the glass of which looked dark in this light, full of shadows. Shadows that might have teeth, should he try to dispel them.

'You're alright,' Albert said softly, and Marcus turned back to face him.

'What did you see?' he asked.

'I think you know,' the old man answered, and stifled a sigh. 'Just don't go lettin' him know I seen him, that's all.'

'So he was up there?' Now Marcus didn't want to look at his window; didn't care if he never saw it again, in fact.

'Oh yes,' Albert said, and shook his head. 'But son, he's been with you a while. Didn't you know?'

And thinking about it, Marcus realised that on some level he had. Those nights when he couldn't sleep for the fear that someone was lurking in the darkness, the burning smell that had made him scared he was having a stroke, as no one else seemed to notice it. And there was the atmosphere in his room.

He'd always been happy there, always felt like it was a refuge, somewhere he could relax. Except lately it had started to feel more like a prison, or a room in a lunatic asylum; full of whispers he couldn't quite hear, shadows he couldn't quite find forms for. The room had felt (*occupied*, his mind whispered, and he nodded in agreement)… like it wasn't his anymore. And he was no longer welcome. Marcus stared at his friend, wondering what else Albert knew. He repeated his question. 'How come you can see 'em, Albert? How come it's just you?'

Albert said nothing at first, just leaned back in his chair and watched Marcus from beneath half-closed eyelids, his expression carefully blank. Then he sighed, and rubbed his eyes as he answered. 'First of all,' he drawled, 'we're not entirely sure it's just me, or are we?' He paused for a moment, but went on when he saw Marcus didn't know. 'And second of all, the reason I can see him, and the others, is an old one. Can you think of it?'

Marcus stared, his mind a blank. Who knew a good reason for seeing dead people? Unless… 'Did you ever die, just for a minute, Albert?'

Albert roared with laughter. 'No, son; not even a little bit. Think harder.'

Marcus did. He sat staring at Albert, eyes wide, listening to the sounds of the street without even realising that he was. He could hear children shouting with laughter, a mother calling her child to heel, people muttering further back in the café, somethin' about fools and being careful what you wished for.

He jumped. Albert was watching him, not laughing now, and to Marcus it felt as if the temperature had dropped a good five degrees, maybe more. Slowly, he turned his head and peered through the plate glass window into the café's interior. It looked gloomy in there, from out in the sunshine, and Marcus couldn't see anyone at first. Then he started to see details in the gloom. A hat here, the set of someone's shoulders there. There were maybe two or three people sat close to the window, basking in the sunlight, chatting away about the usual minutiae of the everyday. Further back, though, it was different. Three figures sat together against the back wall, and one more stood at each side. Those were men, Marcus thought; too tall to be women. The seated figures were female, though, he was sure. They had hats, and sat with bags on their laps, hands clasped on the straps to hold them safe. All five were staring back at him, and belatedly Marcus realised not only could he see what they were, he could see right through them. He cried out, and turned back to his friend for an explanation.

'Can you see…' he whispered.

"Course I can,' Albert replied. 'They're nothing to worry about, just here to watch the world go by – and maybe keep an eye on you.' He sat forward then, and now he was deadly serious. 'They want to make sure their great white hope is safe, you understand?'

'Great white hope?'

'Uh huh.' Albert was all business now, any humour he'd shown before quickly forgotten. 'I can see them, Marcus, because I have the gift of seein'. I'm the seventh son of a seventh son, and believe me, *all* those tales are true. You, though,' and here he stopped, chewing on his lip as he turned to stare into the café's interior. 'You have the gift because of that damned harmonica. And it *is* damned, you can trust me on that.'

Marcus found that he did indeed trust Albert. On everything. He'd known from the start that there was something special about it, but that was all just surface, he knew now. It was special because it held some aspect of its previous owner close to it; they existed in some kind of strange symbiosis, and now it was his, Marcus realised he'd inherited a link with the creature, too.

'So if I get rid of it,' he asked, and there was a marked quaver in his voice now, 'it'll all go away? I won't be able to see things like *that* (and here he gestured with a slight nod at the café's shadowy inhabitants) anymore?'

'I don't know for sure,' Albert replied, 'but that would be my guess. That thing wants something from you, son, I know that much. What I don't know yet is what that is.'

Marcus thought about it. He knew what that thing wanted, at least in part; he wanted the people Marcus raised to be brought to him. What he didn't know was where that meant he had to take them, or why. Deciding that perhaps Albert might be able to help, he cleared his throat and started to tell him everything that had happened.

He could see Albert's eyes growing wider as he spoke, shocked both at the appearance of the creature demanding the raised souls be delivered, and also at the fact that Marcus' mother seemed to be attempting, at least, to intervene.

Finally, when all was told, Albert signalled to the waitress, holding a finger to his lips as he stared at Marcus all the while. When the waitress came, Marcus kept quiet, curious as to what Albert was up to.

'Honey,' Albert said with a smile that seemed just a little off, somehow. Too wide, too bright – it didn't match his eyes. 'I would like a bottle of your finest brandy, please, and two glasses.'

Her eyes widened. 'But that's going to cost…'

Albert interrupted, the smile a little smaller, the tone a little shorter. 'That's fine,' he said, 'just you go on and bring it. Quickly now.'

The girl nodded, crestfallen. 'Yessir, I'm sorry if…'

'No need to be sorry,' Albert said, his tone a little smoother once he knew the brandy was coming, 'we're just thirsty, is all.' He waved his hand, dismissing her, and she scampered off back to the safety of the kitchen.

No sooner had she disappeared than she was back, face shocked as she balanced a bottle of brandy and two glasses on a silver tray and wove through the tables to reach them. Albert put a ten-dollar bill on the tray and waved her away, shushing her gasp of thanks as he told her to keep the change.

'You flush all of a sudden?' Marcus asked.

Albert grinned. 'It sure looks that way, don't it?' He busied himself opening the bottle, pulling its cork with his teeth before spitting it out onto the pavement and pouring a stiff measure of liquor into each glass. He nudged one across the table to Marcus and, nodding at him, took a swig of his own before going on. 'Truth is, I always keep a ten-dollar bill safely stashed in case of emergencies. Never know when it's going to come in handy.' He took another deep swallow of brandy and coughed. 'And I'm starting to think this is an emergency, aren't you?'

'I guess so,' Marcus answered, suddenly convinced that thing was back up in his room, watching the two of them drink and talk in the sunshine. Hearing every word. He turned slowly, glancing over his shoulder towards his apartment window, but nothing was there. Nothing he could see, at least. 'So what do I do?'

'I don't know,' Albert said, 'at least not yet. I'd suggest that for now you carry on playing, carry on living, try and figure out a bit more about who he was, his background, if you can. Think you can do that?' He leaned forward at this last, intent on Marcus' response. Marcus realised more hung on his answer than he probably knew.

'I think I can,' he said, nodding slowly. 'I mean, I know a little bit, but we do need to know more.'

'Tell me what you do know.'

So Marcus did. When he was finished, Albert poured them both another generous slug of brandy and downed his in one, gesturing for Marcus to do the same. Then he poured them another one.

'We might know who he was,' he said, and now Marcus could smell the booze on the other man's breath. 'But we need to figure out how he did what he did.'

Marcus was starting to feel woozy; he wasn't as hardened a drinker as Albert seemed to think. He sipped the brandy slowly now, breathing deeply, feeling the contents of his stomach gently roll. It was not a pleasant sensation. 'So where do we find the information we need?'

Albert thought about that for what felt like a long time. 'Well,' he said, 'there's the library; they keep old newspapers and such, going back years.'

'And if they don't have anything?'

'Son,' Albert said, and now he was sober, all semblance of drunkenness gone, as if it had never been there to start with. 'You'd better pray that they do.' He stood, heaving his not inconsiderable bulk out of the chair with surprising grace, and leaned down to whisper his next words into Marcus' ear. "Cos if they don't, we're talking getting into some serious shit.'

With that he turned to leave, looking back at Marcus with a wink as he said, 'I'll see you tonight, youngster. Be ready to play your ass off; there've been rumblings about finding a new member of the band while you've been away. Need to show 'em who's boss.' Then he was gone, leaving a stunned Marcus staring after him as he tried to digest that last bombshell.

Seven o'clock, and Marcus found himself wandering up the road towards the club, the harmonica wrapped in a white linen handkerchief burning a hole in his jacket pocket as he dawdled along. He did not want to play tonight; hell, if it was on that thing he didn't think he'd ever want to play again. And yet he had promised Albert, and he'd never broken a promise. Not ever.

The club loomed in front of him, and he was surprised at how quickly he'd reached it when he'd been actively trying to delay his journey. The lights on the hoarding twinkled brightly and he could see a few people trickling in, ready for a night's entertainment. He swallowed, and his stomach leapt. He hoped that was all they got.

Ron, the bouncer on the main door, nodded at him as he walked up the steps, but said nothing. Marcus didn't know what to say about his absence and figured it was none of Ron's business anyway, so he just nodded in return and walked on by, his head down. No one spoke to him as he wandered through the club's foyer and aimed right, towards the door that led through to the dressing rooms and manager's office, and he found that he was glad of it. He felt exposed out here, every nerve alive and jumping, the skin at the back of his neck crawling as he imagined what might be watching him. He opened the door to his own dressing room in a state of anxiety, hoping the others wouldn't have too many questions about his time off 'sick'.

No one spoke. They were all there, and turned as he came in, but to a man they just nodded and turned away again, intent on their own preparations for the evening's set. Marcus stood by the door for a moment, uncertain of his reception – were they mad at him, or just busy? – and then Albert waved him across to the empty chair beside him.

'Hey Albert,' he said as he sat down and stared into the mirror. He looked a wreck, haggard and sick, so maybe they didn't need to ask any questions, at that.

'Evenin',' Albert replied, patting at the sweat on his face with a handkerchief before rubbing some talcum powder between his palms and gently patting that onto the sweatiest spots in an effort to dry them out. 'I told the guys it was flu, but you're better now.' He stared at Marcus, concerned. 'You *are* better, right?'

'Yeah, yeah, I'm better.' Marcus took his handkerchief out of his pocket and unfolded it, placing the harmonica on the counter in front of him as he dabbed at his own face. He swallowed at the dull thud as it tumbled onto the wood, and dabbed a little more. 'Don't I look alright?'

Albert chuckled. 'Not even close.'

Ten minutes later they were both wearing their white jackets and dress shirts with the little bow ties, and still sweating. They stood and followed the others out towards the stage, listening as they muttered amongst themselves. They'd barely acknowledged Marcus save to inform him the set hadn't changed, and to grudgingly welcome him back.

'Aren't you forgetting something?' Albert whispered as he held the door open. He gestured over Marcus' shoulder with a frown.

'Oh shit.' Marcus turned back and picked up the harmonica, feeling slightly sick at its touch. It was already warm and felt oily in his hand, but perhaps that was just him sweating. He rushed through the open door into the hallway, hoping the evening might pass without further incident as he followed Albert up the corridor to the stage.

Fat chance.

Ten minutes into the set Marcus saw his first 'shade' of the night. He didn't know if that was the right name for them or not, but it seemed to fit. They weren't as solid as the real, physical audience. They stood in shadow, half-hidden, at times barely even there. And only Marcus and Albert appeared to be able to see them. First one to show herself was his mother, standing off to one side of the stage with her old worn navy coat, a hat hiding her eyes – although Marcus thought he caught the odd gleam from them. She said nothing, just stood there, watching her beloved son play that damned harmonica. People danced around her, and once even *through* her, but she didn't seem to mind. She kept her eyes on Marcus, and he thought that maybe she was waiting.

The next figure to show himself was a stranger. Marcus hadn't seen him before, as far as he could remember. The man was short, bursting out of a too-tight black suit and white shirt, buttons straining to hold the cloth over his vast stomach. He was balding, a few strands of hair straggling over his shiny head, and dear Lord was he sweating. He looked to Marcus as if he was on the verge of melting, like a stick of butter left out in the middle of June. This man stood just in front of Albert, and he looked as if he were about to bust from pride. He stood smiling at Marcus' friend, nodding to the music, and Marcus noticed a curious thing.

Albert was furious. He stood there, playing the clarinet as usual, face shining under the stage lights. But he was doing his best not to notice the little man in the front row; he would not look at him. Once, Marcus managed to catch Albert's eye, and the glare he caught made him turn away, embarrassed. After a couple of songs the shade seemed to take the hint; he moved further back, stood off to one side and watched the people dancing instead. He looked crestfallen, and Marcus found himself almost feeling sorry for him. The music came to an end, and as Earl took the microphone to introduce the next song, Albert made his way across to Marcus and hissed: 'Don't pay him any attention!'

'Who?' Marcus asked, careful to keep it quiet.

Earl glared at them both, nonetheless, and Albert made a pretence of wiping his face, speaking softly under cover of that huge white handkerchief. 'My pa,' he whispered, 'don't pay him any attention, please.'

Marcus nodded, shocked. Albert said nothing more, just made his way back to his usual position as he started to play the next song.

Marcus found he was playing on instinct, barely aware of what he was doing. But his body knew.

Regardless of what was on his mind, of how scared he was, his mouth kept on blowing and he kept on finding that tune.

There were more now: men, women and children, all swaying softly to the music, all gazing blankly back at Marcus with gleaming eyes as he stared terrified at them. Albert wouldn't look anymore. He was concentrating on keeping his gaze either on the floor or on the ceiling, unwilling to see what stood in between.

They came to the last song, and Marcus wished his fellow bandmates could see what was happening right in front of them: his mother was standing at the side, shaking her head and wringing her hands. She was mouthing something, but Marcus couldn't make it out. There was no sound, just the sight of her lips and teeth moving desperately as she tried to... what? Pray? Tell him something, warn him? The others were standing in a group now, all clumped together at the centre of the ballroom but in the back, watching the night's proceedings without making a sound. All except Albert's father. He was back in front of his son, unnoticed by the people around him, and he was crying. Great fat tears rolled down his face, and his shoulders shook as he sobbed. As Marcus watched, the man reached a hand out towards his son, but Albert only took a step back and shook his head almost imperceptibly. The man hung his head and turned, then he was standing surrounded by the others, who'd closed ranks around him as if offering comfort. Marcus wondered if they really could.

As the strains of the last song faded away, the air grew darker around the last stragglers in the ballroom.

Marcus watched as people shivered, or reached for their loved one's hand and hurried on their way, eager to reach the safety of home.

That darkness solidified, and now there was a smell of roasting meat; Marcus could almost hear the crackling of flames. His tormentor was back, and he was grinning at Marcus, arms open wide as he approached, white teeth blazing away in that dreadful maw as he came.

Marcus felt himself detach. It was an actual, physical sensation, and he understood at once that he was going crazy. Properly crazy, and pretty soon the men in white coats would come and haul him off to the state mental hospital, where he'd end his days sobbing in his room, begging them not to let Louis in to see him. He felt his consciousness float off, up and to the right, until he was hovering above himself, watching the goings-on below with a detached interest that seemed downright peculiar, but also something of a relief.

'*You know what I want,*' Louis whispered, and raised his eyes to Marcus'.

'You can see me up here?' Marcus whispered, amazed that he was right, he *had* floated up out of his body.

'*Of course I can, stupid.*'

He raised his arm and clenched his fist, and Marcus writhed in agony. He could *feel* it! His insides felt as if he was being squeezed in a vice, his stomach pushed up into his lungs so he could hardly breathe, and he could hear a pulse pounding away inside his head like a big bass drum. He tried to speak, to beg the creature that had been Louis DuPaul to stop, but he couldn't do more than gasp like a dying fish.

Louis laughed, then, the sound grating and full of ash. Then he opened his fist and dropped his arm, and said, *'enough.'*

Marcus felt himself slam back down into his body. He fell to the floor, gasping and wheezing, and tried very hard not to be sick as the smell of burning flesh surrounded him, reached down his throat and filled his insides. He sat up, eyes watering, and realised that the others had left, seemingly with no clue anything was amiss. Something stirred at the edge of his vision and he amended his first thought. Albert had stayed. He was hiding, that was true, but he'd stayed in the room and was watching. Mirroring his father's actions, Albert's lips were moving, quickly and without any sound that Marcus could hear. He was praying, Marcus realised. He'd never known Albert to do that before, and that terrified him more than anything else that had happened up to now. If Albert was praying, then things really must look bad.

'What... what do you want?' he gasped, and cringed when Louis just laughed and leaned closer in so he could whisper. The smell was awful, and Marcus thought he might just throw up right here, in front of him.

'I told you,' the thing whispered, *'I want what's mine.'*

'I don't understand,' Marcus answered, and that much was true. He gestured at the shadowy figures and felt his heart sink as they in turn cringed, shrinking back from Louis. 'What makes them yours, and how do I give them to you anyway?'

He felt, rather than heard, his mother wail at his words, and he looked across at her, tried to smile, to put her mind at rest. Surely she could see he was looking for answers, for ways to help her and the others escape this... *thing?*

'*You can't help them, boy,*' Louis grated, and Marcus jumped. '*They're mine, now and forever. That was the deal.*'

'The what?'

'*You heard me, so shut up and listen.*' Louis reached out and hauled Marcus up by his shirt front until he was hanging inches from the creature's face. Dark eyes still burned in those charred sockets, and they glowed with a life that had no business being there. '*They were mine,*' he said. '"*We believe you," they said, when I said I loved them; but they lied. They set fire to my house and let me burn, me and mine, just so they could go back to their dull lives and forget I ever existed.*'

'But I don't understand,' Marcus whimpered. 'Why would they say that?'

Louis roared, and Marcus echoed his cry as his mind was invaded with a series of images that told him exactly why.

There was Missy, standing outside a store staring through the window at a dress Marcus knew she would never have worn, at least not where she'd be seen by anyone who knew her normally. It was a deep red silk, not the kind of dress a married woman would be wearing. He could almost hear his mother tutting in his head.

He saw a man come up to stand behind her, pressing against her and running an arm around to rest on her stomach. Missy tensed, then realised who it was and leaned back, relaxing into his embrace. It was Louis DuPaul, leaning down and kissing her neck in broad daylight, right where anybody could see.

He saw Louis and Missy dancing now, the room smoky and full of people pressed up against each other as they swayed on the dancefloor. They were slick with sweat, and the heat wasn't only from the room.

Missy and Louis again, naked, and he would have given anything to be able to look away. This was his mama's friend, for God's sake. They writhed and moaned, and now both turned and stared straight at Marcus, who took a step back.

Then he was watching Missy as she argued with her husband, arms up as she tried to fend him off as he came at her with a leather belt, furious at what she'd done. Louis, Marcus wasn't surprised to see, was nowhere to be seen. He saw Missy fall to the ground, screaming as her husband's foot collided with her stomach. She doubled up in pain as he walked out, cursing.

She started to bleed.

There was Marcus' mother, standing in a line to buy groceries, Louis behind her in the queue. Marcus saw him bend down, whisper something into his mother's ear as his hand grazed her shoulder, and he smiled as he watched his mother turn around and call Louis out, slapping him hard around the face for his impropriety.

There was his mother again, walking home, laden with groceries. She walked alone, head bowed and leaning into the strain of the weight she carried.

There was Louis, slinking along behind her, his face dark as a thundercloud. They came to a quiet stretch of road, no one to be seen for miles in any direction, and Louis moved forward, looming up behind Marcus' mother like a nightmare come home.

Marcus saw his mother lying on the ground, grocery bags on the dirt beside her, their contents spilled onto the road. Louis was nowhere to be seen, but there was blood trickling down the side of his mother's face, and her eyes were unfocussed, her lip puffed up and split. Marcus groaned as he saw her dress was rucked up, deep scratches on her thighs. She reached down, straightened her skirts and tried to stand. It took her a couple of tries, but she made it, and then she had to bend down and start retrieving the groceries that man had made her spill. She got them all together and stood up straight, wincing and taking a deep breath before stumbling homeward, her head bowed.

Marcus watched as she entered the house, listening for sounds of anyone else being there, and the look of relief on her face when she realised she was alone. The bags went on to the kitchen table, braced this time against falling over, and she made her way through to the bathroom and shut the door. Marcus heard her crying, and watched as she reappeared in her bathrobe, arms full of her dirty clothing, which she put into the hamper by the kitchen door. She'd scraped her hair back off her face, and washed the blood away, but there was no hiding the bruising to her mouth and cheek.

Marcus watched his father come in, and the tears as she explained that she'd fallen and hurt herself, her pain at the lie evident even to him. His father said nothing, just sat her down and made her tea, but Marcus could see he knew the lie for what it was, and felt guilty for her desire to protect him. It was obvious he had his own ideas of what had happened and didn't really want to know more. He wasn't a violent man, and he'd have felt compelled to seek justice on his wife's behalf, whether or not she wanted it.

Marcus recognised the expression in his father's eyes, the self-loathing and the pain, and realised this attack predated his earliest memories. This was the look he'd always known, and always thought was his fault. Now he knew better. And perhaps… he quailed at this thought, but it persisted… *perhaps he had another reason to hate his son.*

More images followed, showing the other figures he'd seen in the club but didn't know – and all involved

Louis and his spite. Whether it was him romancing a married woman, or beating up on some young guy while his girl watched, just so he'd look good (in his own head, at least) and get the girl, all of them involved Louis hurting someone or leaving disaster behind.

Then it was over. Marcus sat on the floor, gasping for breath, vaguely aware he'd pissed himself at some point while Louis was showing him what he'd done. He chanced a look over at the side of the room. Albert was still there, hiding behind a column, clearly terrified. But he hadn't left him alone, and Marcus was absurdly grateful for that small show of solidarity from his friend. He hoped Louis hadn't subjected Albert to his own show, but suspected he'd reserved that pleasure for him alone. He forced himself to sit a little straighter and took a deep breath, coughing as it burned his throat. Had he been screaming, he wondered? Had he screamed when he saw Louis rape his mother?

The creature that was all that was left of Louis smiled, small flecks of charred skin flaking off and dancing down toward the floor as he spoke. *'See?'* it said, its joy at sharing its hate clear now. *'I gave them my love, and what was my thanks?'* Now the smile disappeared, and Louis loomed over Marcus as he roared, *'Look what they did!'*

Marcus fell to the floor as he was assailed by a new series of images. He saw his father, and Missy's husband, and some other men both young and old, all sharing the same look of grim fury as they stalked up the road towards the home of the great Louis DuPaul.

They gathered in Louis' yard, these men, all hate and anger and flaming torches as they stood there, waiting for him to come out.

They didn't have to wait long. Marcus watched as the curtains rustled, someone inside staring out and then pulling the curtains back closed, eager not to be seen. The men outside didn't move, didn't speak; they stood and they waited.

The front door squealed open, and Louis DuPaul stood framed in the doorway, the light from inside the house glowing around him and throwing the men in the yard into stark relief. Marcus watched as the man turned his head, listening, and he was aware of voices behind him in the house. Louis shook his head, waving whoever it was back, and then he stepped forward and shut the door behind him.

'What do you want?' he asked the men assembled before him.

Marcus' father stepped forward, and Marcus was struck again by the sadness of the man's face. He looked beaten, used up and spat out by this life he had forged for himself and his family.

'You know what you did,' he said, and there was a rumbling behind him as the other men nodded and voiced their assent.

Louis grinned at them, puffing up his chest as he prepared to speak. His voice, when he did, was full of glee, like a child who's been allowed his presents early on Christmas. 'I do,' he said, and laughed. 'And you know what? They were lucky! I chose them, chose them all, and we had us a fine ol' time.'

'You chose them,' Marcus' father spat, his voice choked with anger and hurt, 'but did you ever stop to ask if they chose you? Did you ever give a single one of 'em a choice as to whether they went with you?' He was near tears now, his anger taking over and threatening to burst out at any moment.

Louis thought about that for a moment. Then he took a step forward, his smile not so wide, not so... gleeful, Marcus saw. 'Now why in the hell would I want to do that?'

The mask of humour slipped, and they all saw the monster that lived underneath. This man didn't care about niceties like consent, or respect, this man took what he wanted without a qualm. This man consumed *everything he wanted, leaving nothing behind of any use. He reached Marcus' father and stared down at him, leaning forward so far Marcus' father found himself leaning backward, not wanting to give any ground and step back, but not able to stand upright under this onslaught. 'Why should you be the only one she looks at?' he hissed, and now Marcus' father was getting scared. It hadn't beat the anger, not yet, but it was coming up, getting close. 'She's a fine woman, your wife, and she wouldn't even look at me!'*

'She's my *wife!' Marcus' father cried. 'You got no right to do what you did! To hurt her, to...* humiliate *her like that.'*

Louis bared his teeth, almost growling as he asked, 'Did she say I hurt her, is that it? Did she say she hated it? Asked me to stop?'

Marcus' father shook his head, miserable.

'No,' Louis sneered, 'she didn't, did she. And you know why that is, little man?'

Now Marcus' father found his strength. He spoke loud and clear, so everyone heard him plain. 'Because she was ashamed, that's why. Because you shamed her.'

Louis stared at his accuser without saying a word for the longest time. Then he smiled, and stared round at the men behind Marcus' father. He nodded. 'Damn right I did,' he said.

It went quickly after that.

Marcus watched as his father, enraged, raised the torch he was holding and clubbed Louis to the ground with it. The two men fought, rolling around in the dirt like boys in a schoolyard. Then Marcus' father managed to get the upper hand and rolled on top of Louis, one hand reaching for his throat, the other aiming a knife at the man's chest. Marcus saw Louis reach up, clawing at his father's neck. He saw the blood start to spurt, the look of surprise in his father's eyes as he knelt astride Louis. Then he saw the light go out of his father's eyes and watched as he slumped down onto Louis, his own weight forcing his knife down and into Louis' chest, killing him too.

Two more men stepped up to the porch, ignoring the sounds of crying coming from behind the door, and raised gasoline cans up so they could splash it high on the walls and door. They dragged Marcus' father free, and huddled around Louis' body for a moment, then hauled his dead body to the house, throwing him inside. The remaining men stared quietly as Missy Parker's husband touched the torch to the gasoline-sodden front door and clearly and calmly said, 'Go to hell, Louis DuPaul,' as the house caught fire along with everyone trapped inside.

'*Now you know,*' Louis said, and Marcus saw real grief on what was left of his face. '*They took my family away from me. They made them suffer, just like I did.*' He turned away from Marcus, then, and stared at the shadowy figures still hovering just on the edge of sight. Marcus heard a sigh and wondered if that was his mother.

Louis turned back to Marcus once more, and now his face was set. Hard lines etched into his forehead and alongside his mouth, lines of hate, of sorrow. Lines of rage. *'Now it's their turn,'* he said, and then he was gone.

Marcus let out his breath with a sound that wasn't far off a scream, only now realising he'd been holding it back.

Albert came out from his hiding place, sidling into view almost apologetically, glancing around as if convinced Louis was kidding; he was going to pop up somewhere else any second and rip both their heads off.

'You okay?' he asked.

Marcus nodded, struggling to bring his breathing under control. 'I'm alive, so let's say yes.' He struggled to his feet and stars swam. He bent forward and leaned his hands on his knees, forcing himself to breathe deeply for a while as he tried to slow his racing heartbeat.

Albert moved closer. 'I'll ask again,' he said. 'You okay?'

Marcus waved him off, nodding. 'Just a bit winded is all; give me a minute.' He waited for the world to solidify again, for the floor beneath him to feel like he could rely on it, painfully aware that he was gasping like someone in the grip of an asthma attack. His heart was thudding hard enough that it seemed like it would burst out of his chest any second. Gradually, his breathing became more regular, and his heart slowed down. He was feeling a little better, although he was going to have one bastard of a headache any time now. He stood up, belatedly noticing that Albert was gone. Marcus was surprised at the pang that gave him; he'd thought he could rely on his companion, but maybe all this (whatever this was) had been too much for him.

A door clicked, and Marcus smiled as he recognised Albert padding across the floor towards him, a glass of water in one hand.

'I figured you could use a drink,' Albert said with a shrug.

'Thanks, man.' Marcus took the glass and drained it, relishing the deep cold as the iced water flowed down his throat and into his stomach. The chill was refreshing; he'd been sweating up a storm, terrified beyond measure by Louis as he showed Marcus his own history, and quite possibly what would turn out to be Marcus' future.

He put the glass on a nearby table and stood tall, breathing deep, feeling almost normal now. Standing there with the lights up full, he felt a little embarrassed. There was no doubt that Louis was real. The way Albert was staring anxiously around the room was evidence enough of that. But he clearly expected Marcus to deliver the souls, or spirits, or whatever they were – of his mother, her friend and the others – to him. He wanted them to suffer, as they'd made him suffer, and he wasn't going to wait forever. But how did he do that, even if he could bring himself to? There had to be a way to outsmart Louis, to save the revenants that came to see him every time he played and send that bastard back to hell, where he belonged. Marcus nodded, and became aware that Albert had stopped gazing around the room like some kind of terrified rabbit. He was staring at Marcus now, but the expression on his face was just the same.

'You're going to stop it, aren't you?' he asked. 'Tell me you're going to stop it.'

Marcus sighed, bone weary. 'I'm going to try,' he said. 'I wish I could promise it'd work, Albert, but I promise I'm going to do my best.'

Albert thought about that for a moment, his shoulders bowed, staring at the floor. Then he looked back up, and his face had aged almost a lifetime. 'Well, then,' he said, 'I guess that'll have to do; at least for now.' He turned to face the door and started to walk, pausing only to call over his shoulder, 'You coming, or what?'

'I'm right behind you,' Marcus answered, his voice as firm as he could make it. And he realised that he did, in fact, plan to stop Louis. He couldn't let that monster have his mother, or her friend, or any of the others Louis had shown him. He didn't know how he was going to beat him yet, but something in him knew that he would. *Or die trying*, his mind whispered, and he shook his head. He wasn't going to listen to any of that. Destroying Louis was going to be hard enough without being defeated by his own fears. He squared his shoulders, took a deep breath and walked after his friend. First, they had to get out of here, then they could talk about what was to be done next.

An hour later they were sat in Marcus' room, talking about what to do. They'd been going round and round on the subject but had made no headway so far. The bulb was swaying a little, making the shadows jump and dance. Marcus found himself hoping that was all it was. After his encounter with Louis, he could no longer be entirely sure.

'Are we going to die?' Albert asked, his voice quavering just a little as he finished that sentence.

Marcus shook his head. 'No, man, we're not gonna die. I won't let that happen.'

Albert looked up, his eyes now brimming with unshed tears. 'You don't know that,' he said. 'How are you going to stop that thing if it decides we belong dead?'

'I don't know, man,' Marcus replied. 'But there has to be a way to beat him. There *has* to.' He thought about it for a moment, then brightened. 'Have you ever used a Ouija board?'

Albert froze. 'Hell no,' he said, 'and I ain't about to start now!' He held up a hand to stop Marcus' protest. 'Hold on now, I'm thinkin'.'

Silence reigned. Marcus sat and watched his friend struggle with the problem of how to find out Louis' weakness, and felt sad that he'd destroyed Albert's happiness. Because that was what he'd done, alright. Albert had always been a joker, ready with a one-liner that could crack Marcus up in seconds, or just sitting at the back of a crowded room watching the party go on around him, laughing at people's craziness, as he called it.

At last, Albert stood and placed his hands against the small of his back, leaning backwards in a long stretch and groaning loudly as he did so. 'Dear God, that's better,' he said, and when he looked at Marcus the old twinkle was back in his eyes. No sign of tears now. 'No Ouija board, okay?'

'Okay,' Marcus replied, wondering what Albert was up to.

'But we do need to talk to your ma, at least,' Albert went on. 'We're agreed on that, right?'

'Ri-gh-t.'

'Then what we got to do is obvious; can't you see?'

Marcus shook his head, wondering over his friend's excitement at the prospect of contacting the dead. Who got excited about something like that?

'What we need,' Albert went on, in a tone that suggested he was talking to an infant, and a slow one at that, 'is a medium.'

Marcus sat, stunned, thinking about how to reply. 'Oh, is that all?' he managed eventually, as he rubbed his eyes and then rested his head in his hands. 'All we need is someone who can talk to dead folks, is that right?'

Albert nodded, slightly less delighted now he could see Marcus' reaction.

Marcus was scared. It was one thing having his mother appear in his room (regardless of whether or not it was really Louis in disguise, he thought, but wouldn't say out loud), it was quite another going to a stranger and trying to initiate a conversation himself. What if what came through wasn't his mother? What if she couldn't help at all? All these thoughts and more rushed through his mind as he tried to figure out how to explain his concerns to Albert. Albert who stood there smiling at him, the expression on his face that of a teacher proud of a student who's managed to do their homework correctly.

Albert's smile faded, replaced by a look of concern. 'Are you okay, Marcus?'

Marcus shook his head, angry now in spite of himself, and he didn't quite understand where that was coming from. 'No, Albert,' he whispered, 'I'm not okay. I'm very far from it, in fact. This is crazy!'

'Is it any crazier than what we just saw ourselves, in the club?' Albert asked. He bent down now, leaning into Marcus' ear as he whispered, 'It's not dangerous, Marcus; I know someone. It'll be okay.'

Marcus sprang to his feet, forcing Albert back so fast he nearly fell over. The man steadied himself against the wall, puffing as he wiped the sweat from his brow with a creased handkerchief. 'Who do you know, Albert?' he shouted. 'Who the hell do you know who could do something like that?'

Albert sat down on the bed, his breathing ragged. He sounded like an asthmatic in the middle of an attack, and his colour wasn't good at all.

Marcus was ashamed of himself. He went to the bedside table and picked up the little flask of water he kept there, poured some into a glass and handed it over. 'Here,' he said, his voice gruff. 'I'm sorry, man, I didn't mean to scare you.'

Albert laughed, except it turned into a cough, and it was a good minute or two before he could catch his breath enough to answer. 'I know you didn't,' he said, and took Marcus' hand in his own. 'It's just… seeing that thing in the club rocked me, that's all. Took more out of me than I thought.'

'Are you okay now?' Marcus asked, half-poised to go for help still.

Albert nodded. 'I'm okay,' he said.

It was a lie, and they both knew it, but Albert's colour was starting to come back and his breathing was a little easier, so Marcus was prepared to hold off on the cry for help for a little while. He sat on the bed beside his friend and put an arm around his shoulders. 'Ain't we a pair,' he said, and both men laughed.

'So,' Marcus asked, once they were both on a steady keel. 'Who is this miracle-worker?'

'My ma,' Albert answered, rubbing his eyes as he started to breathe a little deeper. 'She's always had the sight, just didn't like to advertise, you know?'

Marcus nodded. 'I can imagine. Can she really do it, Albert?'

'Oh yeah, ain't no doubt about that.' His face darkened then, and he looked so sad that Marcus didn't press him further. Some stories didn't need to be told.

Nothing more had been said that night, at least nothing of consequence, but a day or so later Marcus was walking up the road with a man who'd turned out to be his best friend, at a time of his life when he didn't think he'd ever have one.

'Is it much further?' Marcus asked. It was a cold day, wintry even though it wasn't yet October, and he shivered as he pulled his threadbare coat more tightly around him. He'd felt feverish the last day or so and wasn't sure if he actually was sickening for something or if it was just his body's reaction to be being permanently shit-scared. He kind of hoped it was the latter, as if Albert was right then they'd be rid of Louis soon enough.

Albert was trudging ahead by a good fifteen feet, head buried in the pulled-up collar of his coat, hands deep in his pockets. It looked to be a much better coat than his own, Marcus thought, wishing he could afford to buy a new one, maybe a couple of sweaters.

Now Albert half-turned so that he was looking back at Marcus, impatience written all over him. 'Nearly there, brother,' he shouted over the wind, and his voice was almost lost before it reached its intended target. 'Maybe five more minutes?'

Marcus waved him on and leaned into the wind that was trying hard to take his feet out from under him. 'You go on,' he yelled, and he forced himself to keep going. 'I'm right behind you.'

At the end of the street Albert took a left, and as Marcus rounded the corner he saw they'd reached the very edge of town. This next turn wasn't so much a road as a track, dirt packed down hard but no paving. To their right was open land, sparse scrub that backed onto trees in the distance. Albert was trudging up the road towards a collection of bedraggled-looking buildings in the distance, barely more than shacks. Two or three of them, and by the looks of it only one was occupied, a thin thread of blue smoke rising from the chimney, promising at least warmth.

As they got closer, Marcus saw the curtains to the left of the front door twitch; someone had been watching their approach. It was a sorry-looking excuse for a home, he thought, and blushed as the shame rose in his chest. Who was he to judge? His own childhood hadn't exactly been flush, now had it.

The front door opened with a creak, and Marcus saw an emaciated woman of maybe seventy standing in the doorway, one hand on the handle as she watched them draw near.

'Albert? That you?' she called, then stood back as Albert nodded and raised a hand in greeting. The tension was back as she viewed the stranger approaching her door with her son. 'And who's this?' she called. 'Is he safe?'

'He's safe, Ma,' Albert replied, and there was a world of weariness in his words. 'He's my friend, Marcus.' Albert had reached the steps now, and climbed them slowly to stand on the porch. 'He needs your help, if that's alright.'

Albert hugged his mother, then, and moved her gently back into the front room so that Marcus could get into the house.

As Marcus walked into the front room, the first thing he noticed was the heat – it was like being hit by a wall of warmth. His nose started to run and his eyes watered. He felt a little like he was suffocating as his lungs tried to make the adjustment from the frigid air outside. He started to cough, and Albert pulled him further in before moving behind him to close the front door and trap the heat inside.

'You okay?' Albert asked.

Marcus nodded, reaching into his coat pocket for a handkerchief and blowing his nose hard. 'I'm fine,' he answered, 'just thawing out, that's all.'

Albert's mother smiled at that, though she was clearly still wary. She moved off towards the kitchen at the back of the house, calling over her shoulder, 'I'll make some tea. That'll warm you both right up.' Then she was gone, leaving the two men to stare around her home.

The room was large, but drafty – the curtains riffled every so often in the wind, lifting right up in the heavier gusts before settling back down. The glass was grimy, Marcus saw, and the wallpaper faded and even worn through in places. The fire burned bright, though, and the lamps dotted about the room gave it a homely feeling. It didn't matter that the furniture was a bit battered, the curtains and even the rug on the bare wooden floor threadbare. It was clean, almost gleaming – Albert's mother took a pride in her home, such as it was, and Marcus determined to show respect. It wasn't easy living like this, he knew that much from his own childhood. All you had was your pride, and without that you were in a sorry state indeed.

Albert's mother came back in, carrying two mugs of tea. They were plain white enamel, chipped, but she carried them as if they were her best bone china. She handed a mug to each of them, then went off again in search of her own.

'Sit, sit,' she said, shooing them both over to the sofa as she re-entered the room, hands wrapped around her own mug. 'Now what can I do to help you, young man? What do you need to know?'

'To know?' Marcus asked, nervous suddenly of confiding in this fragile little woman. It was dangerous, that much he knew. Did he have the right to put her in harm's way? This was a mistake. He should leave. He leaned forward, ready to put his mug on the coffee table and stand, but stopped when she spoke.

'That's for me to decide, young'un,' and her voice was soft as silk, but strong.

'What is?'

'Whether this is dangerous.'

Albert started at that, sitting forward and staring at his mother. 'How do you know it's dangerous?'

'I don't, yet,' she said, smiling. 'But judging by your reactions, I'm not wrong, am I?' She took a sip of her tea, sighed, and placed her own cup down on the table. 'I could see the worry of it on your face,' she said to Marcus, 'that's all. It didn't take any mind reading to see that, I promise you.'

'Still,' Marcus said, and now he felt calm, almost as if what was going to happen next was already written. 'I wouldn't want to see you hurt, ma'am.'

She chuckled. 'Ma'am, is it?' She looked over at Albert, still worried as he sat beside his friend on the overstuffed couch. 'I like this one,' she said, and laughed out loud. '*Ma'am*. It's been a while since anyone called me that, I can tell you that for nothing.' She chuckled to herself for a moment more, tickled at the polite manner of the young man sat before her, then she closed her eyes and grew still, appearing to listen. 'Oh, it'll be dangerous, son,' she muttered, and her voice was deeper now, dirtier, as if she lay buried in the muck and it was forcing its way down her throat, strangling her as it filled her airways and choked her to death. 'You can rely on that.'

Marcus said nothing, just waited. He laid a hand on Albert's arm, knowing that Albert was one step off shaking his mother out of her trance and dragging Marcus out of there. He loved his mother, that was clear, and he was more than half-sorry that he might have brought danger to her door.

'My name's Violet,' the woman said, staring at Marcus now with eyes that seemed to see straight through him. 'Did Albert tell you that?'

'No, ma'am,' Marcus replied. 'He didn't.'

Violet stared at her son, her expression thoughtful. 'I know you call me Ma, or Mama,' she whispered, 'but this boy can call me Violet. He's a good boy; he can call me by my name.'

'Yes, Ma,' Albert said. His voice was full of tears. He wiped his eyes, lips trembling, and whispered 'you stay safe now, you hear?'

'I'll try, son,' she whispered back, and now her voice was so sad Marcus wanted to cry. 'But it depends on whether he lets me.'

'Me?' Marcus asked, shocked.

'No, child,' she said, and chuckled even as a single tear welled up over her eyelid and started its slow slide south. 'I mean *him*.' She gestured over Marcus' shoulder and he froze. Slowly, he turned his head, aware of the tendons creaking and the voice in his head screaming at him to run, run, get out of there!

There was nothing there. He was staring at an empty space, just between him and the front door. There were no unexplained shadows, the lamp provided weak but warm light… and yet…

And yet he could feel something, couldn't he? The hairs on the back of his neck were standing proud, and he felt a soft breeze, deathly cold, playing over the exposed areas of skin – his face, his hands. He turned back to face Violet, but she was gone.

His mother was sitting in the chair opposite his, and she wasn't smiling. She leaned forward, fixing him with those iron-grey eyes that had always freaked him out, and hissed, *'What are you doing here?'*

'I… I'm asking for help,' he stammered, the need to piss overpowering. 'I want to know what to do.'

His mother scowled, but sat back. She gestured at Albert. 'He can't see me,' she said, 'if you're wondering. He just sees his mother, same as always.'

Albert might not be able to see, but he could hear. He was staring at Violet, open-mouthed, his breath fast and shallow. 'Mama?'

Marcus put a hand on Albert's arm. 'Your ma's not here right now, Albert. Mine is.'

'Yours?' Albert's mouth snapped shut, and he sat back with his hands clasped together and started to pray.

The Violet that was really his mother laughed. *'Now he's a good boy,'* she said. *'Wish you'd been like that.'*

'I wasn't so bad, was I?' Marcus asked, trying to remember what he could have done to make his mother think so little of him.

She gave him an appraising look that made him feel knee high, and said, *'not when you were small, no. You couldn't wait to get out though, could you?'*

'What was I supposed to do, Ma? You were gone, Daddy was gone… I was on my own.'

'*You could have kept the house,*' she said.

'That shack?' Marcus asked, and laughed. 'Mama, I hated that place. All it held were memories of how hard things were for you, and for me. Memories of Daddy, and…' Words left him, then, and he choked the tears down.

His mother nodded. '*I can understand that,*' she said.

'I love you, Ma, always did.'

'*I know. But son, if you don't fix this then you, Albert, Violet… half the town could die. Once Louis is finished with us, that is.*'

'Well then,' Marcus said, and drew in a deep, shuddering breath. 'You need to tell me what to do.'

'*What to do?*' Her image was flickering now – Albert's mother Violet seeking dominance once more.

Marcus raised his voice, wanting to make sure she heard him clear. 'You need to tell me how to stop him.'

His mother sighed. When she spoke, her voice was weary, as if she'd laboured for centuries rather than appeared to her son for a few moments. '*You have to go back home,*' she said, every word an effort now. '*Can you get back to the house, son? Can you do that?*'

Marcus swallowed. 'Sure,' he said. 'I didn't sell it or nothin', Ma, I just left. It's empty, has been for a few years now.'

She nodded, and a tear welled up in Violet's eye. '*Then go home, son. You'll find what you need there.*'

'I will?'

That nod came again. '*Go look in my room,*' she said, and now he could barely hear her at all. '*Go there, and you'll find what you need.*'

Violet coughed, shook her head, and asked, 'What happened?'

Just like that, she was back and Marcus' mother was gone. He felt the shock of her loss all over again, worse even than the day she'd died in his arms.

Violet was watching him, and now her face softened. 'She came, didn't she? Your mama came back to help you.'

Marcus nodded.

'And did she?' Violet asked. 'Did you understand what she told you?'

'I know what she said, and it makes sense, sort of,' Marcus replied. 'But what I don't know is why.'

'Hold on.' Violet closed her eyes, lifting her face towards the ceiling.

Marcus watched as her eyes raced from side to side beneath the lids while she tried to find his mother again. She nodded, the movement so small he wasn't entirely sure he'd seen it, and then she did it again. He was sure this time. He felt relief; he'd thought his mother had given all she had to give, but apparently there was something more. He had to hope so, at least. When Violet opened her eyes again and dropped her gaze back to him, Marcus was shocked to see the level of sadness in them. He was nervous, not entirely sure he wanted to hear what else his mother had to say after all.

Violet sighed and sat back in her chair. She'd aged ten years, at least, in the few moments she'd been conversing with his mother. Her skin was damp with perspiration; she looked feverish, weak. She wiped a hand across her brow and shook her head gently as she smiled ruefully at Marcus.

'I don't look too good, do I,' she said.

'No, ma'am,' Marcus answered, 'and I'm sorry for it, because it's my fault, isn't it.'

'There ain't no fault, young'un,' she whispered, 'but could I have some water?'

'I'll get it.' Albert was up and racing for the kitchen even as he spoke, and both Marcus and Violet started. They'd forgotten he was there.

'Will you be okay?' Marcus asked, ashamed that he'd been the cause of the woman's sudden frailty.

Violet nodded. 'I just need to sleep, is all.'

Albert came back with a tall glass of water, slopping it over the glass's edge as he walked. He handed it to his mother and laid a hand on the top of her head, bent down to kiss her. As he stood up, Violet reached up and took his hand, squeezed it.

'I'm alright, son, don't worry.' She looked up at him then and smiled. 'Just tired, I promise.' She took a sip of the water and then placed the glass down on the table in front of her. She groaned as she sat back once more, still hanging on to Albert's hand. 'I'll sleep tonight, that's for sure.'

She was looking right at Marcus as she said it, and he saw at once what she meant. His eyes widened slightly and she shook her head almost imperceptibly. So she didn't want Albert to know. He dropped his gaze, sad all over again. What was that saying? 'One more sleep until the big one...' People used it for Christmas, birthdays, all kinds of shit, but what it really meant – at least what it meant here, now – was one more sleep. The final one. And Violet wouldn't be waking up anymore.

Albert was watching his mother, his expression thoughtful. He wasn't stupid, Marcus knew, and his next words proved that beyond doubt.

'What's wrong with you, Ma?'

Violet's gaze snapped to meet that of her son. 'What do you mean?'

Albert reached out and touched her forehead, rubbed his fingers gently together. 'You're sweatin',' he said, 'and your colour's bad.'

He gestured at her figure, and she pulled the front of her dress tight in her fist, suddenly self-conscious. 'And you're skinny,' he said. 'You've never been big, Lord knows, but now? You're bone thin. What is it?'

Violet sagged visibly. She put a hand to her eyes and held it there for a moment, her shoulders shaking gently. When she looked up again, the answer was written on her face for all the world to see. 'I think you know,' she said. 'I can see that you do.'

Albert dropped her hand and moved across the living room, stood staring out of the window. 'Why didn't you tell me?' he asked, his voice rough with unshed tears.

'What's to tell?' she said. 'Everybody dies, son, and there ain't no cure for what I got. Why scare you before I have to?'

'And now?' Albert turned to face her, and he wasn't holding anything back now. 'Should I be scared now?' His fear was turning to anger, and Marcus couldn't blame him. He'd had no time to prepare himself, no time to get ready to mourn – and by the look of Violet, he wasn't going to get any, either.

Violet shook her head, shrugged her shoulders. 'I'm sorry,' she whispered, 'I didn't want you to be burdened with it.' She took a deep breath and looked her son in the eye. She looked as if her heart should break. 'I guess now it's time to be scared,' she said. 'Like I said, I'm sorry.'

Albert turned and stormed out of the room, slamming the kitchen door shut behind him. Marcus and Violet sat there, staring at each other, listening to Albert's sobs as he tried to get his head around what his mother had told him. The wind had risen, and rain was pelting against the shack's windows, making them vibrate in their frames with the force of it. Marcus shivered as a draught found him and pulled his coat tighter. It felt like the end of the world.

'So,' Violet said. 'Do I have to ask you?'

'Ma'am?' Marcus looked at her, not sure what she was asking – or not asking – and when he saw her eyes he knew, and felt ashamed she felt she even had to ask that much. 'No, ma'am,' he whispered, 'I'll look after him, I promise.'

She nodded; that was good enough. 'Well then,' she whispered, wincing as her son slammed his fist into something on the other side of the door, 'I guess you want to know what your mama said, huh?'

Marcus wasn't sure he did.

Violet carried on as if Marcus had assented, her tone matter of fact although the words coming out of her mouth were anything but. 'She told you to go home, didn't she, to look in her room.'

Marcus nodded.

'But she didn't tell you what to look for, did she?' Violet went on. 'She thought you'd know.'

Miserable, Marcus looked at the floor, not wanting Violet to see he was almost ready to cry with shame. He should have known. Once, they'd been close, he and his mother. Once, they'd told each other pretty much everything. And then he'd grown up, or thought he had, and was too good for cosy chats in the kitchen of their meagre home. He wanted to be out there, living, experiencing everything for himself.

And then she was gone.

Too many times he'd told himself he hadn't abandoned her; he'd had to go out into the world, find his way... when in reality he'd felt hemmed in, the poverty of his upbringing an embarrassment even though he knew how hard she'd worked – how hard both parents had worked while his father was alive – to make sure he was fed and clothed as well as they could manage. He'd always had shoes, and a coat... so what if sometimes they were hand-me-downs or from the thrift store? He'd been warm and dry; he'd never gone to bed hungry – and he was pretty sure he couldn't say the same of his mother. She'd gone without so many things to make sure her boy didn't suffer, and what had he done? He'd high-tailed it out of there just as soon as he could find work. And it wasn't even that great a job. He played in a two-bit band in a two-bit club for not much more than pocket change, most of the time. He lived in a bedsit apartment in a rundown boarding house and called it independence.

He thought again of the conditions his mother had ended her days in, and thought he might be sick at the injustice of it. She'd deserved better than a son like him, that much was certain.

'Hush now,' Violet said, and there was a hint of fire in her tone. 'Your mother wouldn't want you to think like that, son. Everyone has to make their own way in this world, and there's nothing to be done about that. You did what you thought was right, and who's to say you were wrong?'

I am, thought Marcus. *I'm pretty sure I did wrong by my mother, alright. Just when she needed me most, I up and left.*

'*Yes you did,*' Violet said – except it was his mother's voice once more.

Marcus looked up, and saw her leaning towards him, her expression fierce as his mother's eyes blazed out of her face.

'*You left me,*' she hissed, '*but it was the right thing to do and don't you forget it. You hear me? There was no work near home, I knew that; and I knew you wanted to play music for a living. How were you going to do that round home, boy? You **had** to go; I know that. Now stop wasting time and go get that bastard.*'

Marcus stared, his mouth working hard but no sounds escaping. In all the years he'd lived at home, or since, he'd never once heard his mother swear.

'What is it, son?' The voice was Violet's once again, his mother gone for now, at least. 'What did she say?'

Marcus couldn't answer. He stared dumbly back at her as she closed her eyes, appeared to listen, then nodded and smiled.

'Maybe you can stop blaming yourself now,' she said when she opened her eyes once more. "Cos you're the only one who is, you know. You need to remember that, Marcus, and move on with your life. Make her proud.'

'How do I do that?' Marcus asked, the shame of his lack of success rushing back in on him, the heat of it rushing up through his body and into his face until he was sure his cheeks must be pure scarlet.

'Just live right,' Violet answered, 'that's all, ain't no secret. Don't lie, don't cheat, you know the rest. But first…' and here her face dropped, the weight of what she was about to tell him clearly showing in the sag of her shoulders, the frown lines on her brow. Her eyes were wet when she looked at him next. 'First you got to destroy that son of a bitch.'

Albert laughed, and both Marcus and Violet started. He'd been quiet for ages now, and they hadn't heard him come back into the room.

'And how do we do that, Ma?' he asked bitterly. 'What do we do, pray him away? Have you *seen* how strong he is, what he can do?'

'You know I have,' she said, and the steel in her tone stopped him in his tracks. 'Now hush and listen.'

'Your ma didn't say what this thing you have to find was,' Violet replied. 'She just told me you'd know it when you see it. It's small, and old, but you'll recognise it for what it is.'

'And what's that?' Marcus asked.

'A talisman of some kind,' she said, 'what you might call a charm. It has the power to break his hold, to let the souls he's calling go free, back where they belong.'

'To heaven?'

'If you want to call it that,' Violet said. 'They'll go on to their resting place, where they belong. And he won't be able to do anything to stop them, or anyone else. You won't have to worry about him coming after any of 'em, or you.'

Violet stood then, and Marcus wondered if she realised she'd wiped her hands on her skirt after letting go of his. As if she'd touched something dirty and wanted the scent of it off her hands.

She saw him looking and grinned. 'Not you, young'un, don't you worry. Ain't nothing wrong with you.' She turned and made her way back to the kitchen, started banging cupboard doors and rattling tins.

She returned with a parcel of waxed paper in each hand, and shoved one at Marcus and one at Albert. 'Sandwiches,' she said. 'You'll need something to eat.' She also had two bottles of soda in the front pockets of her apron, and she handed each of them one of those, too.

She gestured towards the front door. 'Go on now, you've got a walk ahead of you if you want to get home by daybreak.'

Marcus stared at her. 'You want us to go out in that?'

'In what?'

She was right. Marcus realised he couldn't hear the wind anymore, and no rain was smacking into the side of the shack. As he stared towards the window, Marcus realised dawn was breaking; the windows were showing the first signs of the night lightening, even though the sun was a way off just yet.

'Go home, Marcus,' she whispered. 'Your mother's waiting.'

Half an hour later, Marcus and Albert were trudging up a sodden dirt path, their feet squelching in the mud left by the night's storm and their breath steaming out in front of them to show their way. The drinks and sandwiches were long gone, finished within minutes of leaving Violet's home. The air was chill, heavy with moisture, and the sun had yet to show its face. Instead it was sulking, hiding behind a mass of low-lying iron-grey cloud that felt as if it were following them, step for step, as they made their way back to Marcus' home. Not an auspicious start to a visit, not by a long shot.

Albert's mother had been right. His mother was waiting. Marcus could feel it more with every passing mile, and with that knowledge came fear of what she would tell him.

After an hour of misery, Albert finally put a hand on Marcus' arm and pulled him to a stop. 'Wait.'

'What? It's not far now,' Marcus answered, not wanting to hear what his friend had to say. He was fairly sure he was going the last mile or so alone.

'I know that,' Albert said, 'I can see it on your face. But we need to talk.'

Marcus sighed, fidgeting as his eyes flitted every which way but towards Albert. He didn't want to see his friend's departure in his eyes. He needed him.

'Look at me, dammit.'

Marcus looked at his friend, steeling himself for the worst. Albert was smiling.

'What's so funny?'

'You, you idiot. Why wouldn't you look at me?' Albert knew damn well, that was plain, but he was going to make Marcus squirm and nothing was going to dissuade him.

Marcus stared flatly at his friend for a moment, unwilling to give him the satisfaction of sounding like an idiot. He was beginning to realise the dread had come from their foe, not his friend. 'I thought you were going to say you had to go home,' he grudgingly admitted.

'What the hell would I do that for, now of all times?' The smile on his face was vying with incredulity now; unable to believe what Marcus was saying.

'I thought...' Marcus fell silent but could see he wasn't about to be let off the hook. 'I thought you were too scared, is all.'

Albert frowned. 'Have I said or done anything to give you that impression?'

'Well no, but...'

'But nothin',' Albert said, his tone brooking no argument. 'That wasn't what I wanted to say, but I bet I know why you thought it.'

'You do?'

'I'm guessing our friend wants you alone,' Albert went on, 'and good and scared. You'll put up less of a fight that way.'

Marcus nodded, feeling the truth of it. 'I guess so. So what was it you wanted to talk about?'

Albert stepped closer, almost whispering as he went on. 'I wanted to ask you about your ma.'

Marcus froze. 'What do you mean?'

'I know my ma said she'd help us,' Albert whispered. 'And I believe that. But do you have any idea how? Any idea what's at that house that you don't already know about?'

'No, I don't,' he answered. 'But she was a good woman. Hard, you know, but she knew right from wrong.'

'You don't think...' Albert said, and stopped. Marcus watched him as he struggled to put what he was feeling into words, and the feeling of dread that had started to lift a little slammed back, full force. 'You don't think maybe it was lyin'?'

'What was?' Marcus asked.

'Whatever was talking through my ma,' Albert said, and the need for reassurance burned off him like fire.

Marcus shook his head. 'No, man,' he said, and it was his turn to smile. 'That was my ma, I'd know her anywhere. That message your mama gave me? It rang true as anything, sounded just like her.'

'But isn't that what...'

'Isn't that *what*?' Marcus snapped, and he was getting angry now.

'Isn't that what the devil – 'cos that's what he is now, and we both know it – isn't that what the devil would say? Play like he was your ma and flat out lie to you?'

Marcus laughed. 'Shit, Albert, what are you trying to do? Scare me to death?'

Albert smiled at that, but his eyes were mournful. 'Marcus,' he answered, 'if you ain't, then you're stupider than I thought you were.'

Marcus laughed at that and turned his gaze towards the road again. 'You know,' he said, 'you might be right at that.'

The two men trudged on in silence for a while, the sky darkening as they went, the sense of warning increasing with every step, but still they put one foot in front of the other, and still they headed towards Marcus' childhood home.

When it finally came into view, the first thought to cross Marcus' mind was how small it looked; how *shabby*. It was barely more than a shack, he saw now; this house that had seemed so sturdy when he was a child. The roof looked like it needed more than a little attention and there were shutters hanging lopsided at the windows, hinges blown out by some storm or other. There was a burnt smell around the place that he couldn't identify the source of, and he wondered what had happened here since he'd gone.

The yard was gravelled over; that was new, and Marcus wondered when that had happened, who had done it. It had been raked recently, he could see that much, but the whole place had an air of abandonment. No one had lived here in some time, probably no one since his mother had died. He felt a pang at the memory of missing her funeral, but hoped she'd understand. He couldn't have faced seeing her get put in the ground, dark and cold for the rest of time. He didn't ever want to think of her like that. He didn't think his heart could take it.

Unbidden, his mother's face came into his mind, flesh almost gone, eyes shrunken and muddy in her head. She turned to stare at him, and that awful mouth cracked open as she grated, *'Son…'*

He flinched.

'You alright, Marcus?'

Albert's voice, normal and kind, almost undid his resolve right there and then. He shivered, and nodded as he answered, 'Yeah, I think so. I think…' he looked around, felt the air of expectancy around them, and continued, '…I think whatever's here is playing with me. I saw my mother.'

Albert's voice was closer now, right behind him, his breath warm on Marcus' neck. 'That's a good thing, though, right?'

Marcus laughed. 'You think?'

'Well sure,' Albert said. 'What's bad about seeing your ma?'

Marcus turned to stare at his friend, his gaze flint as he snapped, 'Depends on if she looks dead, I guess. What do you think?'

Albert paled. 'She looked dead?'

'As a doornail,' Marcus said, and now the anger was gone from his voice. He just sounded tired. 'Her…' and here he struggled to find the right word, '…her flesh was mostly gone, and her eyes were all flat like a dead fish or something.'

'Shit.' Albert's voice wobbled as he went on, 'You're right, I'm sorry.' He gazed around, eyes wide, and whispered, 'Is she here now?'

Marcus had to laugh. 'No, she's gone,' he answered. 'You can stop searchin' for her.'

'Praise Jesus,' Albert whispered, making the sign of the cross as he continued to stare around the yard. 'So what do we do, go inside?'

A door banged in the wind, and both men jumped. The house stared back at them, blind, its dark windows seemingly uninterested in whatever promise they thought they might hold. A gust of wind pushed them forward, and both men staggered a step or two closer to the door. Now they were here, both were reluctant to go any further, at least for now.

'Still want to go inside?' Marcus asked, smiling at his friend.

An embarrassed grin was all the answer he got; all the answer he needed, really. Neither of them wanted this, but they had to stop Louis before he got what he wanted, before he condemned his killers to an everlasting night, bound to do his bidding for the rest of time. He couldn't let that happen to them. They'd done wrong, true, but they'd been trying to put things right when everything went south. That had to count for something.

'*Does it?*' something whispered in his ear. '*Are you sure about that?*' And Marcus wet himself, right there in the yard in front of anyone who cared to see. Whatever it was (it was Louis, he knew it was) chuckled, and the air around Marcus seemed warmer for a moment. It smelled of oranges, and something flowery, and he knew his mother was with him. '*Go on and change, child,*' she whispered, and he sighed with relief. '*Your things are still there, you know that.*' Then she was gone, and Marcus was standing in piss-sodden trousers in the front yard of the house he'd grown up in, sobbing like a lost child.

'What is it?' Albert asked, and touched his arm gently. He was staring at Marcus as if he thought he'd fly up like a rocket if he made too loud a noise or touched him too hard. 'What is it, are you alright?'

Marcus wiped his nose on his sleeve and nodded. 'I think so,' he muttered. 'He was here, that's all. Scared me.' He stared at the house and felt the misery well up inside him; tears threatened once more but he would not let them fall. The time for that was past now. 'C'mon,' he said, his voice unsteady, 'let's get inside out of the cold. I need to change.'

Albert said nothing about the fact he'd wet himself, and Marcus found himself absurdly grateful for that one small act of kindness. He just nodded and started off towards the house, gravel crunching wetly under his feet as he went. 'C'mon, then,' he said, 'it's gonna rain again any time now.'

The front door was creaky as hell, and Marcus found himself resolving to oil it once this was all over. He realised he was planning on moving back in, making it home again, and had to smile. All those years he couldn't wait to get away, and here he was planning on decorating, making repairs so it was cosy once more.

They found themselves standing in a small front room, and to Marcus it felt as if he'd never been away. The bare floorboards were covered with a rag rug just in front of the fireplace, the sofa arms and backs covered with those little lace cloths his mother had loved so much. What were they called – antimacassars? Something like that. He'd always thought it a stupid name, but his mother had loved it. Said it sounded classy, like something a real lady would have in her home. He was ashamed now that he'd laughed at her for that; angry at her for not thinking herself a lady. She'd been the most ladylike person he'd ever known – quiet and dignified, strong. He'd never known her to drink, or swear, at least while she was alive. She'd kept her home – and her son – clean and tidy. She'd been strict with him, trying to instil what virtue she could in a boy intent on going his own way. He took a deep breath and his nose filled with the faded scent of oranges and flowers. She was here. He looked around, saw the pictures of his grandparents frowning down at him from the wall, his mother laughing, young and carefree – and her favourite painting (print, he supposed) that hung over the fireplace. It showed a beach, with children playing near their families, bright sunshine casting everything in happy tones. You could almost hear the children laughing, the sound of waves lapping on the sand and not a cloud in the sky. He smiled. She'd always wanted to go somewhere like that; she'd spoken about it often. His smile fell as he remembered that she never had. She'd never got that chance.

'What do I need to go to the beach for?' she whispered in his ear, and he felt himself relax. He was home, his mother was by his side. That was enough for now.

Albert stiffened, turning to stare at the air beside his friend.

'You heard that?' Marcus asked, surprised.

'I heard something,' Albert said, still staring like a scared rabbit at the empty space to Marcus' left. 'Something about a beach?'

Marcus laughed. 'Ma's here,' he explained. 'She was wondering why I was so sad she never got to go to the beach.' He gestured at the painting over the fireplace.

Albert stared blankly at it for a moment, clearly still disturbed, then took a deep breath and forced himself to relax. 'It's your mother,' he said, smiling. 'That's not scary, right?'

Marcus' mother, Irene, chose that moment to chuckle from somewhere just behind Albert, and the man jumped forward at least two feet.

Marcus couldn't help it. He started to laugh, the mirth bubbling up inside him until he was doubled over, hands on his knees, guffawing like he was never going to stop. Tears flowed freely down his face, tracking down the lines etched in his cheeks, and every so often he'd wipe them away with his hand only for them to redouble in seconds, or so it seemed. Finally, the laughter tapered off, and he stood tall once more, breath hitching in his chest as he hiccupped himself back to some kind of normality. He felt as if the weight had been lifted off his shoulders, as if he could fight anything now. He sensed his mother's pleasure and realised that perhaps that had been the point.

'Can't beat him if you're scared, boy.'

Marcus turned towards the fireplace, noticing Albert echoing his movement by his side, and saw the air start to thicken just in front of it. There was that smell again, flowers and oranges, and now his mother stood before them. Not quite solid, not quite real, but real enough they could both see and talk to her. Marcus raised his hand, and even before he'd realised what he was doing, his mother shook her head and smiled, her eyes sad. *'You can't touch me, son,'* she said, *'I'm sorry. I wish I could hug you, one more time.'*

Marcus felt a tear well once more, but this time not brought on by laughter. In life, his mother had been harsh but fair – not the most demonstrative of women, but loving in her own way. He would give his soul for a hug right now, one more embrace from this formidable woman who'd shaped his life even as she protected it with a will of iron. Hugs had been rare, growing up, but they'd always been there when needed. Lord, how he needed one now.

'What are we doing here, Ma?' he whispered, his voice gruff as he fought it for control.

'You're here to find what I hid,' she replied. *'It'll win the day, if you can find it…'*

'What is it, ma'am?' Albert asked. His voice was thin, wavery, but under control. He'd mastered his fears, at least for the moment.

Irene stared at them for the longest time. Her eyes were thoughtful, her brow furrowed as if she was really worrying about something. Finally, she lifted her gaze to meet that of the two men, and shook her head.

'I'm… not entirely sure.'

She turned, then, and wandered out of the living room into the hall, tiny as it was. She looked into the kitchen, staring round at the worn paint and chipped tiles, looking at the cupboards as if she could open them with her eyes alone.

'Do you need me to open them, Ma?' Marcus asked.

Irene shook her head, her gaze dropping to the worn floorboards. A frown creased her brow once more, but she shook her head before turning towards the stairs and looking upward. *'Not down here,'* she said. *'Have to go up.'* Then she was gone, floating up the stairs in a manner both Marcus and Albert found disconcerting, to say the least. She reached the top of the stairs and turned to look down at them, smiling.

'*Come on,*' she said. '*What are you waiting for, an invitation?*' She moved out of sight, and they could hear her whispering to herself as she roamed the upstairs hall.

Marcus looked at Albert, realising he must look as terrified as his friend. His eyes felt too big, as if they were on stalks, and he was finding it hard to swallow. He was sweating, he could feel it, but he was chilled to the bone. 'We doin' this?' he asked.

Albert gulped, then nodded. 'I guess we have to,' he said. 'But can I say one thing?'

Marcus nodded, knowing he wouldn't have to wait long.

'Your mother's fucking terrifying,' Albert blurted, then he was off up the stairs, giggling nervously.

Marcus smiled and followed. 'Yes she is,' he answered. 'But you know what? She always was.' He heard a chuckle in his mind and knew Irene had heard them. He also knew she was okay with them being scared; it meant they'd do whatever the hell she told them to do.

They found her in the main bedroom, the door wide open behind her. She was turning slowly in a circle, searching the room as she did so, presumably trying to remember what it was that she'd hidden. She stared at them when they entered the room but said nothing. Instead, she raised a finger to her lips and shushed them.

Marcus realised he could hear something. It was low, muffled as if hidden inside a cupboard or… he saw his mother smile, and the penny dropped. As if under the floor.

'*We found it,*' Irene said. '*Now we can stop him.*'

'What is it?' Albert whispered, and Marcus felt the man shaking beside him. He couldn't blame him; the sound was muffled, barely there, but it kept coming. He realised it was regular, a beat of some kind. He saw his mother nod at him, knowing what he was thinking, and felt his gorge rise.

'His heart?' Marcus said, horrified. 'You kept his *heart?*'

'*You don't know everything, son,*' his mother said. Her tone brooked no argument, the familiar steel coming to the fore. '*We… I… didn't teach you the old ways, but I'm thinking now that maybe we should have. We wanted to protect you, here in this new world. What need of the old superstitions here?*'

She stamped on the floor, hard, and the beat became slower, subdued, as if it were scared of her. When she moved towards them, Marcus realised she had more substance now. She was almost solid in fact, walking instead of floating. He wondered if…

Her hand closed around his wrist and he had his answer. She could touch things now, properly touch them and exert force. But how much?

Irene smiled, and leaned in to whisper. '*Don't make me show you, Marcus. You're a good boy, and Lord knows I love you, but we have to end this thing now,*' she said, gesturing at the floor. '*He needs to go back into the dark, and this time he has to stay there.*'

Marcus moved back under the pressure of his mother's almost-gentle pushing, and Albert kept pace with him. Neither man wanted to argue with her. She'd kept them safe thus far, they had to trust she knew what to do. As the two men stepped back over the bedroom's threshold into the hall, they saw Irene raise both arms and hold them wide as she rose into the air. Her head tilted back and her eyes closed, and she started to whisper.

Neither man could say for sure what she was saying, but the effect was immediate. The air felt charged, full of electricity, and Marcus felt the top of his head, convinced his hair would be standing right up above him as if trying to escape. It wasn't, but he could feel the crackle running through it, and had a feeling it'd be standing on end for another reason entirely before too much longer.

The air was growing darker, thicker. They could almost taste the ozone, the power in that room was so strong. Both men flinched as shutters started to bang back and forth against the walls of the house as the wind rose to screaming speed outside.

Marcus craned his neck to see out the window behind his mother. They might be on the first floor, but he'd grown up climbing the big old oak tree at the boundary of their yard, and at this time of year the leaves were in full bloom. He could see the branches whipping back and forth in the wind, leaves being stripped and flung to the winds as the tree fought to stay rooted in its spot.

He looked at his mother once more, and almost fell to his knees. She was staring right at him and her eyes were pure white, like someone had poured milky water into them, obscuring the iris entirely. And yet she saw him. She was staring right at him, those blind eyes unblinking, and she was smiling.

'*Come here,*' she said, and reached a hand toward him.

Marcus took a step forward, unthinking, raising his own hand to take his mother's. He hadn't gone two steps when a blast of wind broke through the window with a howl, hurling his mother into his arms and throwing them all back into the hall. The bedroom door slammed behind them, and something in there growled in satisfaction. The air was hot now, uncomfortable. Something was on fire, it had to be.

His mother groaned, and in the orange light that now pervaded the hall Marcus saw that her eyes were back to normal, or as normal as they could be. She saw him, and she started to cry.

'*We're too late,*' she whispered. *'He's here, and we weren't ready.'*

Something laughed, the other side of the bedroom door, and the heat racked up a notch.

'He's here? For real?' Albert's voice was high-pitched, thin with fear.

Irene nodded, still prone in Marcus' arms.

'What were we going to do, Ma?' Marcus asked. 'That thing was still under the floor, wasn't it? We hadn't even got it out yet.'

Irene sighed, and Marcus realised she felt lighter now, less solid. He stared down at her, and realised her skin was becoming thinner again. She was resuming her spirit form, little by little, and Lord knew how long she could stay with them; how long she could help.

'*He has the heart,*' she said, and flinched when there was an answering howl from inside the bedroom and something heavy thudded against the bedroom door, causing it to rattle on its hinges. It laughed, and rattled the door handle, but the door held fast.

'*We can still win this,*' Irene went on, '*but it ain't going to be easy now he's got his heart back.*'

'But Ma,' Marcus asked. 'Why did you hide his heart there in the first place? What good did that do?'

Irene shook her head, visibly distressed. She was fading, but not ready to go just yet. *'It took his power,'* she said. *'Haven't you learned anything yet? He'd made a deal, should have been dead long before, and yet there he stayed, large as life and twice as natural.'* She laughed. *'If you could call anything that man did natural.'*

'How?' Albert asked, and flinched back when she glared at him.

'How do you think?' she spat at him. *'He knew magic, is all. He knew how to use it to keep on living, even if others had to die so he could.'*

'Who died, Ma?' Marcus whispered, afraid of what he would hear.

Irene's eyes closed, and she wailed, the sound thin and reedy in the silence of the hall. She was fading still, her body now almost weightless in his arms, but still she held on. *'He took the children,'* she whispered. *'Oh, I know he carried on, and that's why we killed him – or at least that's what was said, but no one ever told the real reason he had to die. Children disappeared, from time to time. At first rarely, but it was happening more and more and he was getting greedier, taking more, moving on from children to girls a little older. Not quite kids, but not full grown, neither. And what he did to them!'*

She wouldn't say any more, but both Marcus and Albert had their suspicions. They found it even easier now to understand why Louis had signed his own death warrant.

'So you killed him by taking his heart?' Albert asked.

Irene nodded. *'We did.'* She opened her eyes once more, stared into her son's. *'Your daddy did.'*

Marcus stared. He barely remembered his father and had never been able to get his mother to talk much about him. *'He's gone,'* she'd say. *'Ain't no cause to talk about it, it won't bring him back.'*

'Is that how he died?'

Irene nodded once more. *'Louis was almost beaten,'* she muttered, her voice muddy with exhaustion. *'He was on the ground, bleeding hard, and your father was down there with him, fighting to get his knife in that man's chest; to get his heart out so we could dump what was left in the house and burn it down, put an end to the misery he'd caused.'*

'But his family was inside!' Albert cried, disgusted.

Irene shook her head. *'I know that's the story, son, but they were already dead. He'd killed them himself, to drain power from them and be strong enough to beat us. He nearly did it too.'*

'Nearly?' Marcus prompted.

'Yes, son. Nearly. He was on the ground, fighting your daddy as hard as he could, while your daddy was trying to take his heart, put an end to it. Louis gouged at your father's neck, opened it right up, and that did for him. He was already bloody, and hurt, almost done in, but he bled out so quick once that beast's nails had opened his throat.' She chuckled. *'Thing was, that's what did for Louis, after all. Your daddy fell down, dead weight, on Louis' chest.'*

'With the blade under him,' Marcus finished for her.

'That's right. Drove it right in, killed him. When the others dragged him off, both men were dead. It was just a matter of removing Louis' heart before he could come back, is all.'

'Come back? He could do that?' Albert was stunned, gazing around suddenly as if Louis might appear at any moment and kill them all.

'Of course,' Irene said, and laughed – though not unkindly. *'Isn't he back now? Hasn't he been bothering you and my boy these last few months?'*

Albert stared at her, dumbfounded, and Marcus watched as the tumblers in his head turned around and everything finally fell into place.

'So now he has it back, he's flesh,' Albert said. 'He's real now, ain't he?'

Now it was Marcus' turn to stare.

'*Give the boy a cigar,*' Irene whispered, and she smiled at Albert. '*You got brains, son.*'

Albert blushed, smiling back at her, and Marcus wondered at how much younger his friend looked, suddenly. He looked as if a weight had been lifted, but he didn't understand why.

'*He has the heart, and that's bad,*' Irene said, '*but we hid something important here, all the same.*'

The growling on the other side of the door, that had been going on all the time Irene had been explaining, fell silent suddenly. Whatever was in there was listening.

It wasn't lost on Irene. She glared at the door, and called, '*Won't do you no good, Louis; you ain't going to hear a thing!*' She whispered something, the words almost musical in intonation, and the air in front of them started to glow – a soft, golden light shimmering around the bedroom door like an insubstantial curtain.

'*He ain't going to hear anything now,*' she said, and laughed. The door shook as Louis vented his frustration, but there was no sound. She was right.

'Ma, how did you…?' Marcus whispered, overawed at this latest display by the thing that had once birthed him, brought him screaming and crying into this life, whether for better or worse he didn't know.

'*Told you,*' she whispered, '*the old ways. Time was, this knowledge was taught to all the children, to keep them safe from the night and what wanted in. Those days are gone now, those monsters forgotten and drained of their power; but that might not be entirely for the good.'*

She forced herself to sit upright, and she was more solid, more there, again. *'That don't matter now,'* she said. *'You have to get the key.'*

Marcus laughed at that. 'A key to what?' he asked.

'Hush your mouth, boy,' she thundered, and Marcus was quiet. He stared at the floor, embarrassed at being pulled up short by his mother in front of Albert, being embarrassed by a *ghost*, of all things.

'I may be a ghost, boy,' she went on, her tone pure vinegar now, *'but I'm not stupid, and don't you go thinking I don't know what I'm talking about, alright?'*

'Yes, ma'am,' he whispered, sulking.

Irene sighed, and stared at him until he dropped his gaze to the floor again. *'Stop your sulking,'* she snapped, *'it ain't going to do anyone any good.'* She waited, and when she was sure there would be no further interruption, she carried on. *'It's an old key; small. Made of bone.'*

Marcus couldn't help but look up once more. He opened his mouth, then snapped it shut at one look from his mother. He wasn't about to interrupt her again, not now. She was on a roll.

'Some say it's a leg bone from a fairy,' she said, *'but I don't believe that. Some say it's a finger bone from a witch, and that I* do *believe. It's small, like I said, and kind of yellow, like a smoker's teeth. So you tell me,'* she said, and now she clearly wanted someone else to talk, to question, *'does that sound important enough for Louis to come back for it?'*

'Yes, ma'am,' Albert whispered, and he pushed backward until his spine was supported by the opposite wall. 'It does. It also sounds dangerous, so tell me again why we're looking for it? Why we'd even want it!'

Marcus interrupted. 'I can get why we'd want it,' he drawled, 'but not how it works. Tell us that, Ma, please? What are we supposed to do with it once we get to it?'

'I'm glad you're scared,' Irene said, *'tt means you'll be careful, as you should be,'* The door shook again and the shimmering light blinked out – just for a second, but Marcus saw the fear in his mother's eyes. She muttered those words again and it brightened, became steady once more. Whatever was on the other side of the door (it was Louis, his mind whispered, though he wasn't entirely human anymore) whined in frustration then quietened down.

'You're supposed to open the door,' Irene went on, *'the one that leads to the other side. That door will pull Louis through it, once and for all, and shut behind him, locking him into whatever hell he's created for himself over the years.'*

'Is that what happens?' Albert asked. 'We make our own death? Our own… place afterwards?'

'For some,' she said. *'You have to realise, son, that that's more of a punishment than most folks know or can even stand. Louis killed lots of people in his time, child or grown, and that made a dark net for him. I don't rightly know how he got back, but if we can return him to the other side…'* She went quiet, then, and stared blankly at the shining door, exhausted. *'Then we can lock the door behind him once and for all with that key, and what comes after that isn't down to us. It's not even our business.'*

Albert and Marcus stared at her in silence, wondering if she'd speak again, but she just stared at the door, her face wet with tears. She'd suffered at Louis' hands, that was clear, but so had Marcus. He'd lost his father before he even had a chance to get to know him, and Louis had come back to torment him purely so he could goad him into helping him regain the souls he'd held captive for so long.

Marcus' eyes grew wide as something occurred to him and, seeing his friend's face, Albert shifted away, just a little, just enough to put some space between them should his mother get angry. 'Ma?'

Her eyes turned back to him, and he could see the sorrow. She already knew what he was going to ask.

'Why did he come back to me, Ma? He didn't even know me.'

'No,' she said, and that word told him everything. *'But he knew me, and that was enough.'*

'So Daddy…'

'Was furious that I'd been hurt, furious that I'd been too scared to tell him…'

'And furious I wasn't really his,' Marcus finished for her.

Irene hung her head and started to cry in earnest. *'No, not that. You were his, alright. But DuPaul hurt me, just the same, and your daddy killed him for it. If Louis hurts you, he gets his revenge over me, can't you see that?'*

He nodded, then his gaze snapped back to the closed bedroom door as Louis thumped against it, and he saw the shimmering was fading fast despite his mother's best efforts. The door was rattling in the frame; any minute now it would open, and Louis would be out – with them.

'I hope you're ready, boy,' she said, and he could see the effort she was expending to keep the door closed just a little longer. *'It's under the crooked floorboard right at the end of the bed.'*

He nodded and got to his feet, absurdly glad to see Albert doing the same.

'You okay, Albert?' he asked.

'Not even a little bit,' his friend replied. 'But I'll keep him busy while you get it.'

'Question is, Ma,' Marcus said as he watched the door, 'what do we do when we get it?'

'Bring it to me at the old church,' she said, her voice so faint he could barely hear her. *'I know where the lock is.'*

Then she was gone, and the door was banging in its frame, the thing on the other side roaring with frustration. With a final bang, it flew open, and Louis stood in the doorway, panting, his eyes blazing as he saw them.

His hands were raw. The deep gouges on the inside of the wooden door showed where he'd done that damage; he'd almost got right through the wood in places. He was bare to the waist, his scrawny torso covered in blood and sweat. His eyes were wild, his hair sticking up and matted with blood where he'd obviously head-butted the door as he tried to get through it.

'Where is it?' he snarled, *'what did you do with it?'*

He stopped and tilted his head, sniffed at the air like a dog looking for a scent, and sighed. *'So that's it,'* he said. *'That bitch helped you.'*

Marcus tried to look innocent, tried not to betray his mother. 'What bitch?' he asked.

Louis laughed. *'Don't give me that. Your mother. The bitch who hid it, who's hiding it now.'*

'Hid what?' Albert asked, joining Marcus. He was trembling; Marcus could feel the shudders rippling through his friend's body but didn't dare try to calm him, either by look or touch. Louis would be on them in an instant, and all would be lost.

Louis was watching him closely. His eyes were grey, the whites yellowish and filled with water. He looked like something long drowned, standing there in front of them. He moved closer to Marcus, sniffed the air around him. He was standing no more than a pace away, and the stench coming off him was terrible. He smelled like spoiled meat left out in the sun, and Marcus fancied that if Louis showed them what he really looked like, this long after he'd been in the ground, they'd both go mad. He'd be rank; what little flesh was left hanging off him in strips, ripe with maggots that squirmed and buried themselves ever deeper, eager for better meat.

Louis laughed quietly, and Marcus knew that the creature had understood every thought that had just passed through his head. How could he not? His disgust was probably written all over his face. He chanced a peek at Albert, and his fears were confirmed. He looked as if he was about to puke, his colour almost gone, his breath coming in shallow gasps.

'I have quite the effect, don't I,' Louis whispered. *'Well this is all your mother's fault, boy. Your ma and her damn fool husband and their friends. If they'd just left me alone I'd have done the same, and none of this need to have happened.'*

He leaned closer, whispered in Marcus' ear. *'All I wanted was a little* fun. *What's wrong with that?'*

'What's wrong with it?' Marcus said, furious now. 'You hurt people. Good people. You don't get to do that. It's not *fun.*'

Louis howled at that, tears of laughter spilling out over those awful pouches under his eyes and splashing down his ruined cheeks. *'Oh Marcus,'* he gasped, when he could catch his breath. *'There's too much of your mother in you, boy. You don't know a damn thing!'*

He reached up and grabbed Marcus' shirt front with clawed hands, then turned and threw him into the bedroom, where he crashed into a heap in the middle of the floor. He followed, turning to shout at Albert over one shoulder, *'You stay there. No one needs you.'*

The door slammed shut, and Albert found himself alone in the corridor, weeping like a lost child.

Marcus couldn't breathe. That was the first thing he realised, lying crumpled on the bedroom floor and staring up at the iron bedframe he knew so well, the water stain still in the middle of the ceiling from that storm when he was nine. He tried taking shallow breaths, almost sips of air, but the pain in his ribs was still bad enough to make him want to stop; to not breathe, to just lie still and let it be over.

'What's the matter, Marcus? Want to cry Uncle?'

Louis. With a groan, Marcus rolled onto his back, fighting the nausea that rushed to meet him as the pain in his ribs racked up several notches.

'Marcus!'

That was Albert, out in the hall. He could hear his friend rattling the door handle, banging against the wood of the door, but he wasn't going to be able to get into the bedroom in time to help him, Marcus knew that. He had to delay whatever this thing standing in front of him wanted to do, but first he had to figure out how to move when he could barely even breathe.

'Look at you,' Louis said, and the disdain in his voice was enough to get Marcus moving. He was slow, an earthworm could probably have moved faster,

but Marcus managed to haul himself into a sitting position and stretch across towards the bed frame. He managed to snag one of the iron posts and hauled on it, groaning as he pulled himself towards the bed, finally reaching it and leaning against the bed's footboard, panting for breath. He coughed and wondered why his mouth was wet. He wiped his lips with one hand, and realised when he stared at his bloody palm that his ribs were going to be more of a problem than he'd thought. He'd poked a lung, possibly in more than one place, and if he didn't finish this soon and get help, he might not make it.

That was a sobering thought, and Marcus stared at Louis for a long time without speaking.

Louis seemed content to wait. There was a smile playing about his lips, he was enjoying himself. He'd discounted Albert, that much was clear, and he didn't think he had anything to fear from Marcus, not in the state he was currently in.

He was probably right, Marcus admitted to himself. There wasn't a whole lot he could do with his ribs splintered and his lungs bleeding every time he coughed. He had to hope that Albert would come through for him.

Sure enough, Albert was still hammering on the door, growing increasingly frustrated at the lack of response. Then he went quiet, and Marcus heard his footsteps tapping away down the hall, muttering to himself as he went.

Was he leaving, Marcus wondered? Had he realised this was too much for him, that he wasn't going to be able to help? Marcus didn't think so; he didn't think that was in Albert's nature – or if it was, he'd never seen any sign of it before this.

'*Sounds like we're alone,*' Louis said, '*we can take our time after all.*'

He moved across the room to Marcus' mother's chair by the window and lowered his gaunt frame into it. He groaned as he leaned back against her favourite cushion, the one she'd made herself, and stretched his legs out before him.

The trouser legs flapped around limbs that were almost bone, precious little flesh left to pad them out. There was a smell around him, almost sweet – the smell of putrefaction, of rot. He grinned at Marcus, revealing several gaps in his mouth where the teeth had fallen out. The ones left looked too long, the gums rotted back almost to the roots of his teeth, the teeth themselves yellowed and feral. '*We can have a chat,*' he said, and laughed.

'What about?' Marcus asked, his ribs singing now, his breath getting shallower. He felt as if his chest was filling up with liquid, and he supposed that might be right. Something inside was bleeding and wasn't going to stop anytime soon. He was in trouble.

'*Bout you and me,*' Louis drawled, staring at him as if he was a bug in a trap. '*Did your mother tell you?*'

'Tell me what?'

'*Who I am? To you, I mean?*'

Marcus laughed. 'You're not my father, if that's what you mean. My mother told me the truth.'

'*Did she?*' Louis asked, his voice soft, and that stopped Marcus cold. He shrugged, and stared at Marcus without speaking for what felt like minutes but could only have been seconds. '*Your dad killed me, you know. Stabbed me right in the heart.*'

'You deserved it,' Marcus spat at him. 'You hurt my mother, you killed my father, and you hurt others besides.' He glared at Louis, furious at his attempts to make himself sound better than he was. 'You took *children*, man, you hurt *kids*.' He shook his head. 'That's a special kind of low.' Then he was coughing, blood spattering his shirt as he gasped for breath.

When he could breathe again and the room swam back into focus, Louis was standing staring out of the window.

'I had to do that,' he said. *'You don't understand.'*

'Oh yes I do,' Marcus said. 'My mother told me; you lived too long, and didn't want to give that up.' He stared up at Louis, and asked, 'What made your life worth more than theirs? Can you answer me that?'

Louis turned to stare at him, and his face was stern. *'Of course I can,'* he said, laughing. *'I had a destiny, and it wasn't just grubbing around trying to grow a few sparse crops, or keep mangy chickens so my kids didn't starve… I was destined for greatness!'*

'Oh you were,' Marcus said, his voice disdainful.

'Damn right I was!' Louis shouted. *'I wanted to build something, to be remembered. I built half this town single-handed, did you know that?'*

Marcus shook his head. 'I don't believe you.'

Louis strode forward, leaned down and hissed into Marcus' face as he went on. *'The people of this town, the first ones, the pioneers… they couldn't find their asses with both hands. I showed them the way! I showed them where to settle, where to dig their wells, where to build their shabby little houses… they'd be dead without me!'*

'That didn't give you the right to feed off them!' Marcus shouted back. 'They were people, families… they had a right…'

'*To what! They had a right to nothing,*' Louis shouted. '*They were mine to do with as I pleased. That was the bargain I made, that was my price for finding them somewhere to settle.*'

Marcus leaned back, stunned. His mother had said that Louis used the old ways to gain power; now he realised fully what that meant. Wandering, lost with a group of settlers, Louis had resorted to magic to find a home – to gain power, and to keep it. It seemed he hadn't had any problem with the price that had been asked in return.

'And if you didn't meet your side of the bargain?' Marcus asked, hoping against hope that Albert hadn't deserted him after all.

Louis stood straight once more, his gaze flitting around the room as if sure something was listening; something that might bite.

'*Then the price was mine alone,*' Louis admitted, '*and I wasn't about to pay.*'

He'd spent the rest of his miserable life making others pay, Marcus saw. It didn't matter who. He had his power, a family that did whatever he said, money… if he had to throw someone else to the wolves now and then, so be it. He was safe, and so were his family. Except that eventually he got lazy, forgot to hide his tracks… or thought no one would do anything anyway. He thought wrong, and thank God for that.

'How'd you find your heart?' Marcus asked abruptly.

Louis blinked, surprised.

'You died, right?' Marcus went on. 'And they took your heart so you couldn't come back. Yet here you are.'

Louis puffed his chest out, pleased at the apparent flattery. '*Here I am indeed,*' he said.

'*I suppose there's no harm telling you now,*' he said at last. '*I mean, there's not a lot you can do about it, is there? They thought taking my heart out was enough; they thought I wouldn't be able to come back without it.*' He ran one long fingernail down his chest, and a line of scarlet opened up behind it.

Marcus choked down the vomit that was trying to escape and tried to look away. He couldn't. He watched as Louis peeled the skin back on both sides of the cut, and opened his chest cavity for Marcus to see. His heart was there, shrivelled and black, stuffed into a cavity that was otherwise empty save for dirt and maggots. The stench rising from that hole was awful, and Marcus leaned to one side and threw up, splattering the floor with blood and bile.

'*But they were wrong,*' Louis went on. '*I could come back enough.*' He turned to stare around the room, taking in its shabby décor and lived-in look. '*Once I followed you here, I could smell it.*' He took a few steps towards the door, frowning, then smiled once more. '*That's all I needed to be able to come back in the flesh. Not having it just meant I couldn't do it all at once, that's all. I had to build my strength, as it were.*'

'Which is why people started to disappear again,' Marcus whispered, thinking out loud, 'and why you started to come and see me.' The harmonica seemed to vibrate, then, in his pocket, and he slapped a hand on it to hold it still. 'The harmonica,' he said. 'Did you send me that too?'

'*Give the boy a cigar,*' Louis crowed. '*You got it in one.*' He cocked his head, listening, and Marcus found himself holding his breath.

Marcus stared at the monstrosity standing in front of him, momentarily lost for words. The harmonica had brought the dead to see Marcus; had drawn them to him. And it had alerted Louis to his presence, brought him back too. Now he was looking for a key made from a witch's finger that would open a doorway and let him rule triumphant. You couldn't make that shit up, Marcus thought. It was crazy.

'Haven't played it for a while, have you?' Louis asked, watching him with what looked like amusement.

Marcus shook his head. 'It's been a few days, I guess.'

'Not since that night in the club, huh.'

Again, Marcus shook his head.

Louis smiled at him. To Marcus, it felt like having a shark open wide so it could bite your whole head off.

'Ain't you curious?' Louis asked.

'About what?' Marcus answered, uncomfortably aware that Albert had come back into the room and was now peeping out from behind his friend. *No protection there*, he thought. *If he wants us dead, we're dead.*

'Don't be so sure about that, son.'

Marcus sighed. So she was still around. Maybe they had a little hope of getting out of here alive after all.

His mother laughed, her voice almost inaudible as she whispered, *'he's just messing with you, that's all. He wants the key, and... I think... the harmonica too.'*

Louis strolled nearer, his air nonchalant as he stared back at Marcus. He leaned forward, sniffed the air between them.

'She's here, isn't she?'

'Who?' Marcus asked, standing firm.

'You know damn well who.' Louis straightened, and now he bared his teeth properly, not even pretending

he was smiling. *'She can't stop me, son. You know that, don't you?'*

Marcus said nothing, determined not to give Louis the satisfaction of hearing the tremor in his voice. He was cold yet sweat ran off him in sheets; his back was slick with it, and it was all he could do not to shiver.

Louis took a step back. *'So be it. I'm bored now, so I'll warn you just once more.'* He was fading, the contours of the bedroom starting to show behind him as Marcus watched. So he wasn't *confined* to flesh, even with his heart. 'I'm guessing you don't know where the key is. Stay out of my way, boy, and let me have it. Or I'll bring you pain you can't even imagine. Understand?'

With that he was gone, and Marcus felt a rush of hot air on his neck as Albert finally allowed himself to breathe out. He felt sick, weak; he knew how close they'd come to being snuffed out like burned-out candles. Louis was getting desperate, and if he thought Marcus and Albert were no more use he'd have killed them both already. He needed them to find the key.

'Marcus?'

Albert's voice was thin, shaking. 'Marcus,' Albert said again, and this time Marcus turned, shocked to see the toll this had taken on his friend. Albert looked ten years older, his face drawn and almost grey, his eyes red-rimmed and watery. He didn't have a whole lot left to give, by the look of him.

'What is it, Albert?'

'What are we going to do?'

Marcus sighed. 'Right now, I'm not really sure.' He took his friend's arm and led him out into the hall, back towards the stairs. 'Tell you what. Let's see if there's anything left to drink. I think we need to catch our breath.'

Ten minutes later they were sitting around the battered kitchen table, hands gripping mugs of coffee – there hadn't been any food in the house, but there'd been a jar of coffee lurking in back of one of the cupboards that looked as if it might still be drinkable, and God knew they needed the warmth. It was bitterly cold in the house, a chill that sapped the strength and will, leaving you longing for respite any way you could get it.

'So what do we do?' Albert muttered, hugging his coffee close to his chest. 'Can we even win now?'

'I don't know, man,' Marcus answered, setting his own mug back down on the table and standing up, stretching. 'All I know is we have to try.' He felt the weight of the harmonica in his pocket and dug it out, held it up to examine properly. 'Wish I knew what this had to do with it, though, don't you?'

'More than you think.'

Marcus jumped. 'Ma?'

Irene shimmered into view. She looked exhausted, but her eyes glowed like fire and golden sparks flew off her every now and then, like fireflies in the darkness of the house's interior. She stared around. *'This place used to be warm, didn't it? It used to feel like home.'* Her lips moved, though neither Marcus nor Albert heard a sound, and then the lamps on the wall were glowing, and they heard a whoosh as the fireplace in the living room across the hall guttered into life – albeit a little unwillingly.

'What... Ma, what did you do?' Marcus asked, awestruck.

Albert had stood up in a hurry, overbalancing the rickety kitchen chair he'd been sitting on, and moved into the living room at a half-run, standing in front of the fireplace with both hands outstretched as he basked in the warmth.

'I forgot what warm was like!' he exclaimed, and Marcus could see steam rising from Albert's shirt and trousers as the chill started to evaporate. Colour came back into his friend's cheeks, and he looked happier than Marcus had seen in what felt like weeks, but really could only have been a couple of days. It was so simple, Marcus thought, to lift someone's spirits. Keep them warm if they're cold, listen to them, and hope rises again.

The house was starting to warm, the heat from the fireplace gradually raising the temperature throughout the small building. Marcus drained the last of his coffee and moved into the living room after Albert, smiling at the man's obvious joy at so small a comfort being restored.

'*Feel better?*' Irene asked, still giving off those firefly sparks, heat emanating from her, too.

'I do, thank you,' Marcus answered. 'Could do with some food, but I guess that'll have to wait.'

'*Guess you can't have everything,*' his mother whispered, amused. '*Now then. Have you figured it out yet?*'

'Figured what out?'

His mother said nothing, just watched him, waiting… and Albert pitched in, 'The harmonica! Am I right?'

Irene turned to gaze at him, a half-smile playing around her lips, but she said nothing.

Marcus cried out as the harmonica twitched in his hand, and dropped it to the floor as if it were red hot.

It lay there, staring up at him, firelight gleaming on the mother of…

'Shit!'

The air around Irene grew darker. The firefly sparks flew higher, she looked angry.

'Sorry, Ma,' Marcus whispered, 'but shit!'

'Boy you better…'

A chord blew from the harmonica as it lay on the rug in front of the fireplace, and both men jumped. Marcus fancied his mother did too, though he knew better than to draw attention to that fact.

'What was that?' Albert shrieked.

'Calm down, Albert, you sound like a girl.'

Albert huffed, but said nothing else, just watched Marcus as he reached a leg out and tapped the harmonica with his foot. Nothing. It lay there, staring blandly up at him, just so much wood, metal and mother of…

There it was. He had it now, he was sure of it.

'Is that…' He stopped, unsure of exactly how to phrase his question.

Irene waited, while Albert was virtually hopping from foot to foot, he was so excited at having figured it out.

'Is that the key?' he asked, and sagged with relief as Irene grinned and Albert clapped his hands together.

'I knew you'd find it,' she said. *'I wish I could have told you.'*

'Didn't you know?' Albert asked.

Irene turned to him, the sparks dimming slightly as she did so. This was costing her effort, they could see; she was a little easier to see through now, and she looked exhausted. She shook her head. *'It's been a long time,'* she whispered. *'When I last saw it, it was a key.*

And the harmonica is Louis', that's true. I'd forgotten that we'd joined the two. The ideal hiding place, we thought.' She smiled widely at them both. *'Turns out we were right.'*

'Not mother of pearl,' Marcus muttered. 'Bone. But how could you even do that?'

'Magic, I guess,' Albert whispered. 'Is that right?'

Irene nodded assent, and said, *'We ground the bone up, mixed it with cement into a paste, laid it down and let it set on top of the mother of pearl. Then we polished it, and set a charm on the thing to hide its true nature.'* She laughed, and went on, *'Apparently even from us. The damn thing still called the dead, but its ruin was part of it now. The rest you know.'*

The fire was starting to dwindle, and so was the light – but both men felt stronger, revived by the heat and this new knowledge. Marcus put the harmonica back in his coat pocket and dug his hands deep in them to keep warm. Albert sighed and put his own coat back on, squared his shoulders and stood by his friend.

'Where now, boss?' he asked.

Marcus considered what they knew, what his mother had told them and Louis had inadvertently revealed. 'I'm guessing maybe the cemetery?' he said.

Albert nodded. 'Sounds fair to me,' he said. 'Is it far?'

'Not really; maybe half an hour's walk?'

Albert sighed. 'Lord, I'm sick of walking. My legs are going to give out before this is over.' Then he wrapped his coat around him a little tighter and smiled at his friend. 'Well?' he said. 'Lead on, Marcus, I'll be right behind you.'

The cemetery proved to be a little further away than Marcus remembered. It was almost dusk when the broken-down iron gates hove into view, the left hanging drunkenly on what remained of its hinges, the right securely attached but with a distinct lean. Sundown was a way off yet, but the sky was dark with storm clouds and the wind had whipped up dramatically since they'd left Marcus' childhood home.

They stopped at the crest of a small hill and looked down on the dilapidated graveyard, probably still half a mile away from them at this point.

'Jesus,' Albert said. 'I hope they don't still use that place; look at the state of it!'

'I think they do,' Marcus answered, 'but just the family vaults that still have some space inside. See?' He gestured towards the left bank of the graveyard, where a few mausoleums were dotted at intervals up a small hill. Dank, threatening places they were, and neither man wanted to get close to them. 'Anyone else gets buried in the new cemetery just outside town, on the north side. You know the one?'

Albert nodded. 'I do. It looks a damn sight friendlier there than here, I'll tell you that.'

'Don't worry,' Marcus said, slapping his friend on the shoulder. 'No family vaults for us, that takes money.'

Albert laughed. 'Never thought I'd be glad to be poor.'

They carried on up the road towards the cemetery, both hoping that the storm promised by those clouds held off until they'd finished their business – but pretty sure it probably wouldn't. One more joy to add to the day's list.

Finally, they came to the gates. Up close, it was clear they were neglected. Covered in rust, the hinges rotted… an equally rusty chain holding them closed.

Or it should. As it stood, with the way the gates were hanging, it was easy enough for the two men to squirm their way through and find themselves standing on the other side of the cemetery's threshold.

It didn't look any better close up. To their right lay half a dozen headstones leaning at the craziest of angles, for all the world as if the occupants interred beneath them had clawed their way out. It was not an image designed to induce ease of mind, and both men leaned forward just to check that the ground beneath those headstones hadn't been disturbed. Lucky for them, Marcus thought, there was no evidence that the soil had been broken – either from above or below – so they should be safe on that front. As they walked slowly forward towards the dilapidated church building at the far end of the graveyard, more ramshackle graves lined the path on both sides. None looked to have been tended anytime in the recent past, and the whole place had a neglected air. It felt sad, abandoned, and Marcus half-wished they'd dig these poor souls up and move them over to the newer, more inviting cemetery outside town. At least there they'd be tended; this place looked to have been abandoned years ago.

Something rustled in the undergrowth off to their right, and Marcus wheeled around just in time to see a thick, wiry tail disappear behind an old tree stump.

'Rat,' he said, and carried on, ignoring Albert's expression of disgust. He felt Albert stepping closer behind him, so close he was almost tripping him up, but he couldn't find it in himself to tell the other man to back off. They were both frightened; it would do no good to let that make them turn on each other when they most needed a friend's support.

'Hope we don't see any more of those,' Albert whispered, and then jumped as more rustling was heard.

'They seem to be staying off the path,' Marcus whispered back, wary of making too much noise and attracting attention. 'Let's just hope it stays that way, eh?'

They continued in silence until they reached the chapel, or what was left of it, and stopped in silence in front of the heavy wooden door.

The graveyard might have been neglected, but the chapel was a very different story. This door was thick, solid, and the hinges were in good condition, as was the heavy bolt holding the door closed. Both the hinges and bolt looked to have been oiled recently; there was no sign of the rust they'd found on the cemetery gates and their chain.

The bolt was slid back in the open position, almost inviting them inside. Yet they hesitated. The atmosphere outside was grim, but here, on the chapel's threshold, it was far worse. There was an unwholesome atmosphere here, as if something had tainted the air at some point – and was still around, polluting everything around it. Marcus looked at Albert, hoping his friend couldn't see how rattled he was; how much he wanted to just turn around and head on home.

'Come on,' Albert muttered. 'We've come this far, after all.'

He was right, and Marcus knew it. He nodded, reached forward and grabbed the hasp of the steel bolt. Cold shot through him and he cried out, pulling his hand away and cradling it to his chest.

'What is it? What's wrong?'

Marcus examined his hand, amazed to see there was no sign of frostbite or burning; his palm and fingers were unblemished. 'Nothing,' he said, amazed. 'It was so cold! I could have sworn it was burned but look!'

He held his hand out to Albert for inspection and was reassured to see Albert's frown.

'That makes no sense,' Albert said. 'I saw the flash.'

'Flash?' Marcus asked, surprised.

'Sure. You touched the bolt, and there was a flash of white light. I thought you'd been hit by lightning at first.'

Marcus stared at the door, immovable and completely uninterested in these small creatures standing before it. 'We have to get in there,' he said. 'That has to be where he's hiding, don't you think?'

'Who said I was hiding?'

Both men stared at the door, stunned. Louis had known all along that they were there; he'd just been playing with them.

'Now what do we do?' Albert whispered.

'Now,' Louis announced, *'you come in!'*

The door swung back, slowly, and the men found themselves staring at an empty church as they'd expected – but well looked after. The floor was clean, swept; the pews had been polished recently, leaving the air redolent of lavender. At the far end of the aisle, Louis waited for them, standing front and centre at the altar.

'Come on in!' he crowed, and started to laugh, holding his sides as he fought for breath. 'I'm sorry, I didn't mean to laugh... but your faces! Oh man, you should see the expressions on your faces!'

He kept laughing, and the two men remained silent, standing at the foot of the aisle as they kept one eye on him and tried to gauge their surroundings at the same time.

It was clean, they knew that much, so someone was looking after this place – for Louis? Nothing seemed to have been tampered with, the holy statues that were dotted along the side aisles of the chapel at intervals seemed to be intact, dust-free, and someone had left fresh flowers in a vase at one side of the altar. There was no sign of anything out of the ordinary, no blasphemous graffiti, no signs of damage… a devoted parishioner, then, someone not willing to let the building go to rack and ruin in the same way the outside had. Were they around still? Marcus wondered. Did they know who or what was inside the place now, what harm it would bring with it? His eyes were growing used to the dim light inside the chapel, and he noticed something that he hadn't seen up to now. Someone had left a pile of clothes on the front pew; maybe it was for charity? Someone deserving of the church's aid, some poor parishioner fallen on hard times?

Then he saw a dark stain on one of the items of clothing; a coat, threadbare and worn. The stain was wet. Louis started to chuckle, and Marcus stifled a cry as he realised what he was looking at – the verger, or whatever poor soul had been keeping this place nice. For what? To end up sacrificed to this… thing that had infested the building?

'Oh come on now,' Louis said, his voice rich and deep. This place gave him strength. 'That's hardly a nice thing to think. Infested. Is that any way to talk?' He took a step forward, and the ground shuddered. Marcus and Albert held their ground, but this new dimension to the fight was terrifying. He made the ground shudder now?

'This place is *mine*,' Louis said. 'Consecrated to me.' He gestured at the huddled corpse on the front seat. 'She just didn't know it yet, that's all. She tried to keep me out and paid the price.'

'Dear God,' Albert whispered, and Louis roared with laughter.

'He can't help you now, fool!' he shouted. 'He's long gone!'

Marcus found himself praying that wasn't true. They were going to need all the help they could get.

'Give it to me,' Louis wheedled, and now he was… Christ, was he floating?… down the aisle towards them. 'It's mine, you know that.'

Marcus shook his head, and tried to step back, but was brought up short as he felt the heavy wooden door against his back. When had that shut?

Albert stood beside him, shaking. 'What the hell do we do now?' he whispered. 'We're gonna die, aren't we? We're gonna die.'

'Hush,' Marcus snapped. 'Don't let him hear how scared you are.'

'Hear? Jesus Christ, Marcus, it's right there in front of him! You think we look confident right now?'

He had to admit Albert was right. It had to be clear that they were scared, and yet Louis didn't try and take what he wanted. He hovered a few feet ahead of them, head tilted to one side as he stared at them.

'I want the key,' Louis said, and now he was done with wheedling. 'I know you have it. *I can feel it!*' He snapped his fingers, and Albert cried out as he was lifted two feet off the floor, struggling to breathe as his throat was squeezed by something Marcus couldn't see.

He doesn't know, Marcus realised. *He doesn't know where it is. And if he can feel it now, it's because it wants to be found.*

'I know you have it!' Louis snapped, and Albert started to choke as the creature increased the pressure on his throat. 'What more do I need?'

'Okay, don't hurt him!' Marcus shouted, holding his hands up in what he hoped was a gesture of acquiescence.

Louis snarled at him, but Albert started to cough, so the pressure had reduced on his poor throat. He was twitching his feet, trying vainly to reach the floor – reach *something* that he could rest his toes on – and ease the pressure further.

'It's here,' Marcus said, and reached into his pocket, trying to mask the item he took out. 'But you have to let Albert go first.'

'Think I'm stupid?' Louis drawled, and shook Albert by the neck like a chicken being sized up for dinner. 'I let him go, you run and I have to go to all the trouble of chasing you down like a damned dog.' He shook Albert again, eliciting a moan from the now semi-conscious man. 'Now give it to me.'

Marcus looked around the chapel, hoping against hope for some sign he had help nearby. He was going to need it. The harmonica was fairly thrumming in his hand now, eager to be let loose and play. He could feel veins of energy running up his arm; an arm that itched to bring the harmonica up to his mouth so he could play, so he could let it loose and make everything burn. He took a step back, away from Louis and his friend, and did what it wanted.

The sound was more than anything he'd heard from it before. The notes soared to the roof of the church, lighting it up with a full, rich sound that made the windows tremble and the floor seem to swell up under Marcus' feet. He couldn't have said what he was playing, only that it was a song that lifted his heart, made him want to cry and hug anyone he loved as if his life depended on it.

Louis roared, dropping Albert to the floor as if he were no more than a doll to lay discarded and unconscious. He was safe for now. He moved towards Marcus, but reeled back when he came up against some kind of barrier. He reached a hand out, confused, only to pull it back hissing in pain when there was a golden flash and sparks flew towards his hand from whatever was protecting Marcus.

Marcus smiled, and poured himself into the music that was reverberating around the church. They were coming, he could feel them. It was almost over now.

His visitors from the club shimmered into view. There was his mother, Irene, front and centre, surrounded by her accomplices in the murder of Louis DuPaul. Sweet little Missy Parker was smiling and nodding at him, the others were focussing their attention on Louis, who hadn't noticed them yet. He was still preoccupied with the pain in his hands, staring at them as if he expected to see a snake firmly attached to a thumb.

Louis looked up as they reached him, and Marcus saw the horror dawn in his expression. He turned to face Marcus, and now his face was pleading.

'They'll kill me, boy!' he begged. 'If I don't have the key, I'm lost!'

'You say that like it's a bad thing,' Marcus answered, and took a step back, further away from Louis and his attackers. His foot nudged something, and he looked down to see Albert lying on the floor beside him. He was conscious now, and had managed to crawl across to Marcus' side. 'Stay there, Albert,' Marcus whispered. 'You're safe there, for now.'

'I'm okay,' Albert said. 'I ain't going dancing anytime soon, but I'm okay. Shook up, that's all.'

The livid purple finger-marks around Albert's throat told a different story, as did the strained attempts at speaking, but he was alive, and his throat seemed to be the only real damage.

'Well stay there till you think you can stand,' Marcus replied. 'Louis is going to be busy for a few minutes, at least.'

Albert glanced across and laughed, then winced at the pain in his torn throat. 'They really don't want him getting away, do they?'

'They' had formed a ring around Louis now and were slowly herding him down the aisle towards Marcus and Albert. Irene was in front, leading the way, and she gestured Marcus to move back.

'*We'll take him where he needs to go,*' she said, '*but you need to keep playing. The barrier won't hold long if you stop.*'

'Where are you going, Ma?' Marcus asked.

'*Where do you think?*' she said. '*The DuPaul vault, up at the top of the hill. The gateway's there; he made it years ago when his family died.*'

She looked down at Albert, and her eyes were kind. '*Can you walk, son?*' she asked.

Albert nodded. 'I think so, ma'am. I just need a minute.'

There was a rumpus going on behind Irene, and she frowned and spat a word that made the barrier shine bright gold for a moment. Louis wailed and fell to his knees, and the little gaggle of revenants stood watch. They were flickering in and out of view as they used their energy to hold Louis DuPaul in place, to herd him to the vault where he'd meet his end so they could rest in peace, at last.

'Play, Marcus,' she called, and staggered as Louis launched himself to his feet and tried to storm the barrier. It held, but the cost was high to his mother and her friends.

Marcus brought the harmonica back up to his lips and started to play once more. He didn't think about what to play, didn't even know what it was, but it had the desired effect. He saw the revenants start to grow stronger, his mother standing tall and holding the barrier steady as the others chided Louis and started to herd him back down the aisle towards the church entrance. He moved to one side, aware of Albert standing at his side, and played on as they wandered past. Louis turned to stare at him as they passed, and the malice in his eyes almost made Marcus want to run.

'Go on,' Albert whispered, 'keep at it, Marcus.' His voice was strained, but stronger, and he looked more in control of himself than he had since Louis' attack.

Marcus nodded and started to walk after the spirits, Albert right behind him.

It was a strange procession, this rag tag of spirits and people swaying in time to Marcus' music. The barrier was holding, gold flashes lighting it up from time to time as Louis ventured too close to its perimeter. The sky overhead was almost full black now, and thunder was growling every minute or so. Irene, Missy and the others were less visible out here, simply darker shadows than those surrounding them, but their effect on Louis was profound. He was a trapped animal, hitting against his cage walls now and then almost as a formality rather than showing any sign that he was seriously trying to escape. The path meandered, and a few times Marcus or Albert slipped, but they did make progress even if it was slow, and soon enough the vault at the top of the hill hove into view.

The black clouds seemed to be centred on it, almost as if it was puffing them out from its half-collapsed roof. The thunder was louder now, and Marcus found himself waiting anxiously for the first fat wet raindrop to splat him in the face. It was holding off so far, at least, and he was glad about that. This day was miserable enough without being soaked to the skin.

They carried on slowly up the hill towards the DuPaul vault, Marcus playing softly all the while. The wind was picking up now, and the rain started to spatter against the gravestones, soaking Marcus and Albert in very short order. The ghosts were lucky, Marcus thought. The rain didn't seem to bother them at all.

Fifteen minutes later they were standing outside the DuPaul vault, Marcus still playing – it was a hymn, now, that he almost recognised, but couldn't remember ever having learned to play.

The DuPaul mausoleum was barely worthy of the name anymore, although Marcus had no doubt it had at one time been the pride of the cemetery, eclipsing its neighbours by some distance. Now, the slate roof looked as if it was caved in at the top, with both sides angling towards what looked to be a fairly substantial hole, letting in the elements to do their worst. There was no sign of a tree nearby that could have fallen on it that Marcus could see, nor any stumps where such a tree might have been removed, but slate tiles littered the ground around the mausoleum and had chipped several of the surrounding gravestones.

There were huge, dark wooden doors to the mausoleum that would have been polished to a gleam in earlier times, and these stood firm, although their condition these days clearly left a lot to be desired. There were gouges in the wood that looked relatively new; the splintered shards of the doors' interior wood showing much lighter against the doors' veneer. The lock was broken, hanging out of one of the doors as if forced, and the doors themselves were ajar. Marcus could see the blackness inside and wanted to run, but he kept on playing regardless.

'*You're doing fine,*' his mother said.

Marcus nodded, grateful for that show of kindness, and watched to see what came next.

Missy Parker was the first to move. She stared over her shoulder just once, at Marcus, and smiled her sweet smile. Then she moved towards the doors and made a pushing gesture with her hands.

The doors flew open, banging back against the outer walls on either side with some force, fresh splinters of wood flying off and landing on the ground before the little group of spirits. A cloud of darkness roiled out, and Marcus and Albert threw themselves to the ground with their hands over their heads, looking up only when nothing landed on them, or started to bite, or crawl in their hair.

The spirits were staring at them, his mother openly laughing at their plight. There was no sign of the cloud from the crypt and, feeling sheepish, Marcus pulled on Albert's arm and hauled them both to a standing position.

'What was that?' Marcus asked.

'Nothing that could hurt you,' Irene answered, *'just some bugs, that's all.'*

Slightly ashamed, Marcus couldn't help but brush himself off, run his hands though his hair, still half-convinced he could feel bugs crawling in it.

'Shit,' Albert muttered beside him. 'This is going to be the death of me.'

Marcus looked around for his harmonica, scared he'd lost it. It lay on the ground a foot or so in front of where he'd sprawled, maybe five feet from his mother and her companions. He threw himself forward and grabbed the harmonica, raised it to his mouth and blew. He sat cross-legged on the ground and played the harmonica; and this time he knew what he wanted to play – one of his mother's favourites, 'Mississippi Swamp Moan'. He saw her smile, saw the strength she drew from it, and was happy. Albert was tapping a hand against his thigh in time to the music, and Marcus could feel the mood lift. They all needed that, he knew. They were at the end of a long and dangerous fight, and it was about to get darker. Sometimes a little upbeat could work wonders.

The cloud of bugs had dissipated and the doors hung wide open, tilting wildly to the sides. Louis was standing in the centre of his prison, head hung low. He didn't speak, didn't look up. He didn't move.

And then the dark interior of the vault seemed a little less dark, somehow. Marcus couldn't see an obvious source of light. There was no lantern, no flame that he could see. And yet it was lighter, if only by a little.

'It's opening,' Irene said, and stood back so that Marcus and Albert could see.

Marcus stood, hauling Albert with him as they moved closer to the mausoleum. They gave Louis and his companions a wide berth, though Marcus was very aware that Louis was glaring at him as they passed him by.

There was a doorway of sorts, right at the back of the vault. You couldn't normally see it, Marcus was sure, but the sun had broken through the thick, dark clouds massed over the mausoleum and was shining down through the hole in the roof. The back wall – all the walls – consisted of big blocks of concrete. Several of these were missing at the back, and where there should have been a view of the back of the cemetery – a stretch of the railinged fence, scraggy bushes and a tall, spindly tree that loomed over the back of the vault like a big spider – there was instead a greyness. Not much of a description, Marcus knew, but that was the only way he could think of to describe it. The air inside the doorway (because it *was* a doorway, he knew that much) was just… grey. It looked as if someone had just painted the concrete to look like a doorway, but there was no depth, no texture, no nothing.

'You're not seeing it right,' he heard his mother say. *'Here.'* And then she touched his head, laid her fingers gossamer-like over his eyes, and did the same for Albert. And when she took them away they could both see.

It was a passage. The greyness had depth now, had texture. It dimmed as it travelled further back from the doorway, and it wasn't empty anymore. Marcus could see shapes in it, shadowy figures both large and small that seemed to be waiting for something.

'They want him back, see?' Irene whispered, and Marcus watched Louis start to struggle, throwing

himself from side to side against the barrier that held him. Marcus could almost feel the impact as he watched the damage it was doing to his mother and her companions. Missy was on her knees now, her face grey and barely there. She was muttering something, her hands kneading together and her lips moving relentlessly as she fought to keep hold of this monster they had contained. Irene was standing fast, feet braced against the onslaught, but she was struggling too, and Marcus knew they didn't have long.

'Let him go!' he shouted, and saw the spirits turn towards him, straining to hold on, maintain their cage.

'Let him go!' Marcus repeated. 'Let me do this!'

'*Son,*' Irene asked, '*what is it you want to do?*'

'I want to force him forward, towards the door,' Marcus answered, blowing chords on the harmonica every few seconds in a last-ditch attempt to maintain some kind of control.

'*And then what?*'

Marcus realised he didn't know. The doorway was something that scared Louis, he could see that much, and he knew that his mother had told him they had to force Louis back through to the other side. Wasn't the doorway their way to do that?

'*We'll let him go once we've got the cage inside the vault,*' Irene said. '*He can't get back out of the vault once he's in there. We can maintain a barrier if it's static; it's holding him at bay while he's moving that's so hard.*' She flinched as Louis launched himself at the barrier as if in counterpoint, and with a gesture threw him backwards. Louis landed on his ass, cursing and bawling at her for all he was worth.

'*The doorway's open,*' she said, and now Marcus could see the strain on her face. The others were barely visible anymore, but his mother was strongest. She was fading, but would be with him for the last. She'd be with him when he needed her, as she always had. *'You can't keep playing for ever,'* she said, and now her eyes were sad. *'We never intended that. You have to hand the harmonica over to the other side, let them take it. Only they can close the doorway. Only they can end this.'*

Marcus stared once more into the darkness, tried to make out some detail in the shapes that stood just the other side of the threshold. 'Who are they?' he whispered. 'How can they keep him inside if we can't?'

Irene swayed, and Marcus was reminded of how tired his mother must be; she'd been the driving force behind luring Louis here and manoeuvring him into the vault. The others had lent a little strength, but there was no doubt that she was the most powerful of them all, a fact Marcus resolved to do some research on once this was all over. If they were still around, that is.

She pulled herself upright, closed her eyes and remained still. When she opened them again she seemed stronger, more together. She gazed over Marcus' shoulder and the bleakness in her gaze tore at Marcus' heart.

Abruptly, Irene turned and gestured towards the vault; the barrier containing Louis surged forward, forcing him onwards inside it. He staggered, and the thing shadowing Marcus and Albert hissed.

Once they were at the threshold to the vault, Louis decided to take his last stand and refused to move over the sill. The barrier hissed and flashed as he fought its restraints, and he screamed more than once at the pain this caused him.

'We've got him, Albert,' Marcus said.

There was no reply. Turning, Marcus saw that Albert had fallen to the ground, as he had, but had been unlucky enough to hit his head on a gravestone that stood at an angle, jutting out over the path. The stone was covered in blood, and Albert lay semi-conscious beside it, one side of his head split open and bleeding profusely.

'Albert!'

Marcus dropped to his knees, pulled Albert into his arms and tried to wipe the blood away as best he could with the handkerchief he kept in his pocket to wrap the harmonica. The wound was deep, and Marcus could see splinters of bone.

'Marcus?' Albert whispered.

Marcus stopped what he was doing and focussed on his friend. 'We'll get help, Albert, we're nearly done here, then I'll…'

Albert smiled. 'Too late for that, my friend.'

'Don't say that,' Marcus whispered, 'we can get…'

Albert's eyes were unfocussed, the right seeming to roll independently of the left. The injury was serious, that was clear. Marcus didn't like to think about the splinters of bone, or whether any bone had impacted inward rather than splitting off harmlessly onto the skin surrounding the wound.

'Too late, Marcus,' Albert said, and his breathing was thick, heavy. 'Too late for me. But I can still help, I think.'

With that his eyes rolled back and he lost consciousness; his body lolled heavily in Marcus' arms. Try as he might, Marcus couldn't revive him, and he wasn't altogether surprised when he heard his mother.

'*He's gone, son.*'

Marcus looked up, furious now. 'What more is it going to cost, Ma? Do I have to die too?'

'*No,*' his mother said, and were those tears that Marcus saw in her eyes? '*You're going to be fine. We'll see to that.*'

'And what about Albert?' Marcus spat out, his voice muddied by the tears he would not let fall until this was over. 'What'll happen to him?'

'*You'll bury me,*' Albert said, '*and you'll mourn. But you're going to have to be alive to do it, ain't you?*'

Marcus stared. There was Albert, standing beside his mother, smiling at Marcus as if he'd done nothing more than fall on his ass. 'What?'

'*You didn't think I'd just leave you alone, did you?*' Albert went on. '*I can help now; more than I could before.*' There was a pause as he looked around at the graveyard, at his companions, at Marcus kneeling over his body in front of them. Then he smiled. '*And I'm okay with that.*'

Marcus was far from alright with it; but he laid Albert down gently and brushed a hand over his eyes, closing them. He crossed Albert's arms over his chest and made sure he was clean. He could do that much, at least. And he would mourn, too, long and hard, he was sure. But that would be later. After they sent that bastard Louis DuPaul back to hell.

He stood, brushed himself down, and picked up the harmonica once more. He started to play and 'Abide with Me' floated heavenward in an almost silent graveyard. He'd never played it so sweetly, or cried so hard as he played his friend to his rest. From the corner of his eye, he could see that Louis was cowering within his golden cage, all fight gone. He knew he was done. Irene and the others were finally ushering him over the threshold into the vault, and the greyness at the back of the mausoleum was beginning to brighten.

Still playing, Marcus followed his companions inside and saw the spectres inside that gateway. There were men there, women too… and even one or two children, some barely more than infants. All were standing, some on each side of the gateway, lining it in wait for this passing through of the greatest evil Marcus had ever seen, or hoped to again. He came to the end of the hymn and stopped playing, breathing hard, even as the mausoleum door slammed shut behind him.

Irene waved her arm at the barrier and it shimmered out of existence, leaving Louis free. He stood tall, as if ready to fight, but then several of Irene's companions seized his arms and led him forward, even as he struggled, to the doorway's threshold. Spectral arms reached out to take their charge from them, and Louis was pulled through into the darkness, without another word. Missy and the rest passed through behind him, leaving Marcus alone with Albert and Irene.

Irene held out her hand. *'You can stop now, son,'* she said. *'One of us has to close the door from the other side.'*

Marcus stared at his mother, mute with sorrow. He made no move to hand the harmonica over. Not yet.

She smiled at him. *'It's not forever,'* she said. *'You know that, right? If you need me, I'll come. Always.'*

Albert moved a step closer to Marcus, smiled at his friend and put his own hand out. *'I can do it,'* he said. *'I wasn't much use while I was alive, I know that…'*

Marcus shook his head, eager to disagree, but Albert just smiled more.

'I knew it, and so did you,' he went on. *'But that's alright; I was happy just to be there, to help you where I could – even if it was just by being your friend. Because that's important too.'*

Marcus took a deep, hitching breath, and whispered, 'I'm going to miss you, Albert. I couldn't have done this without you.' He handed the harmonica to his friend, glad to be rid of it, and knew that it was Albert's time now to show what he could do.

Albert smiled his thanks and raised the harmonica to his lips. The strains of 'Abide with Me' could be heard once more as he played, and Marcus started to sob as he watched Albert and Irene walk forward side by side and disappear into the darkness. The music faded, and then was gone; the doorway closed.

It was done.

Marcus waited there, sitting in the vault's open doorway, waiting for the weather to brighten so that he could start the long walk home. He smiled as he realised what that meant. Not the room in town he'd been so proud of, with its beaten-down bed and rickety chairs; but the equally decrepit shack he'd grown up in, that was still his by law, and that was waiting for him. He thought about his mother's paintings, and the kitchen that had got so drab over the years, and as the sun broke through the clouds he got up and started to walk, a spring in his step he'd thought lost for good.

He was going home. He had work to do.

Marie O'Regan is an award-winning author and editor, based in Derbyshire. She is the author of three collections of short fiction and a novel, *Celeste*; her short stories have also appeared in magazines and anthologies in several countries, and she is an award-nominated anthologist. An ex-Chair of the British Fantasy Society and the UK Chapter of the Horror Writers Association, she ran ChillerCon UK, which took place in Scarborough in May 2022. Marie is also Managing Editor of PS Publishing's award-winning novella imprint, Absinthe Books.

SHADE OF STILLTHORPE
by
Tim Major

"*It's fair to say that parenthood has dominated my thoughts – and certainly my identity – for the last nine years. While I love my children unconditionally, I'm morbidly fascinated by the idea of parenthood lacking an instinctive bond to counter the difficulties and sacrifices of such a period of life. And I'm afraid of any possible future in which that bond might be weaker.*

Identity is a slippery thing. More than anything, I'm scared of losing it – my own, and those of the people I love. Several of my novels and stories have related to this fear. In Shade of Stillthorpe, *it's quite literal: how would you react if your child was unrecognisable, suddenly, in all respects?*"

Tim Major

A seemingly impossible premise becomes increasingly real in this inventive and heartbreaking tale of loss."

—Lucie McKnight Hardy, author of *Dead Relatives*

"*Parenthood is a forest of emotions, including jealousy, confusion and terror, in Shade of Stillthorpe. It's a dark mystery that resonated deeply with me.*"
—Aliya Whiteley, author of *The Loosening Skin*

blackshuckbooks.co.uk/signature

THE DREAD
THEY LEFT BEHIND

by

Gary Fry

"*The seed of this novella was a single image I'd long had in mind before composition. A young boy standing in a farmyard no longer knowing which hand he led with. That struck me as a promising metaphor for something my conscious mind had yet to catch up with, and indeed it was another few years before I finally figured it all out. By this time I'd returned to my early love of the classic dark novella. Lovecraft, obviously, but also a renewed appreciation of Arthur Machen, particularly his criminally underrated 'The Terror'. In that piece, I was struck by its accumulative, almost investigative structure, the way it drew upon different sources of information to conjure a vision packed with verisimilitude.*

In The Dread They Left Behind, *I wanted to evoke an isolated rural community via the medium of a retrospective first-person narrator along the lines of he who regales us in HPL's 'The Color out of Space'. The difference is that mine is directly exposed to and physically affected by the historical events. Along with all the requisite intrigue and frights, the piece allowed me to explore concerns I have about political extremism. It took a long while to get right -- I tinkered with it for years. But for me it embodies everything I hold dear in the field. Whether it does so successfully, I leave for readers to determine.*"

Gary Fry

blackshuckbooks.co.uk/signature

Also from BLACK SHUCK *Signature*

CHARLIE SAYS
by
Neil Williamson

"I don't know anyone who grew up in the 1970s who wasn't scarred by the public information safety films on British TV. Those tiny, doom-filled dramas slipped in between the cartoons were often only fifteen or thirty seconds long but, by God, they caught our attention. Don't play with matches, or old fridges. Or kites or frisbees, should you happen to be near a pylon or electricity substation. Be careful crossing the road and running along the beach. And also near ponds and lakes, or when swimming in the sea. And never, ever talk to strangers.

And then, of course, there was Protect and Survive. A full set of instructions for what to do in the event of nuclear war. Coming from a time of such existential dread, is it any wonder that those films are now considered a cornerstone of the UK's collective Horror imagination?

I'd wanted to use them in a story for a long time, but the idea lay dormant until I realized two things. Firstly, that there was an element of warding ritual and incantation to them ("Look left, look right…", "Charley says…") reminiscent of folk horror, only in the urban environment rather than the usual remote rural setting. And, secondly, that those films were what Britain was scared of fifty years ago. What I ought to be writing about was what really terrifies me about this country now."

Neil Williamson

blackshuckbooks.co.uk/signature